Felix Dahn

Saga of Halfred the Sigskald

Felix Dahn

Saga of Halfred the Sigskald

1st Edition | ISBN: 978-3-75237-832-0

Place of Publication: Frankfurt am Main, Germany

Year of Publication: 2020

Outlook Verlag GmbH, Germany.

SAGA OF HALFRED THE SIGSKALD

BY
FELIX DAHN.

CHAPTER I.

Nigh upon fifty winters ago, there was growing up in the North a boy named Halfred. In Iceland, on the Hamund Fjord, stood the splendid hall of his father, Hamund.

At that time, so the heathen people believe, elves and goblins still moved about freely among the Northern nations. And many say that an elf, who had been friendly to the powerful Hamund, drew near to the shield cradle of the boy Halfred, and for his first food laid wild honey upon his lips, and said—

> "Victory shall be thine in harping—
> Victory shall be thine in singing—
> Sigskald shall all nations name thee."

But this is a mere idle tale of the heathen people.

And Halfred grew, and was strong and beautiful. He sat often alone on the cliffs, and listened how the wind played in rifts in the crags, and he would fain have tuned his harp to the same strain, and because he could not do it he was filled with fury.

And when this fury swept over his forehead the veins in his temples swelled, and there came a red darkness before his eyes. And then his arm sometimes did that whereof his head knew nothing.

When his father died Halfred took the seat of honour in the hall. But he took no heed to preserve or improve his inheritance. He gave himself up to harp playing and feats of arms. He devised a new strain in singing, "Halfred's strain," which greatly charmed all who heard it, and in which none could imitate him. And in hatchet throwing, not one of the men of Iceland could equal him. He dashed his hammer through three shields, and at two ships' lengths he would not miss with its sharp edge a finger broad arrow shaft.

His mind was now set upon building a dragon ship, strong and splendid, worthy of a Viking, wherein he might make voyages, to harry or levy toll upon island and mainland, or to play his harp in the halls of kings.

And through many an anxious night he considered how he should build his ship, and could devise no plan. Yet the image of the ship was always before his eyes, as it must be, with prow and stem, with board and bow; and instead of a dragon it must carry a silver swan on the prow.

And when, one morning, he came out of the hall, and looked out over the Fjord, towards the north, there, from the south-south-east, came floating into Hamund's Bay a mighty ship, with swelling sails. Then Halfred and his house-churls seized their weapons, and hurried out either to drive away or welcome the sailors. Ever nearer drove the ship, but neither helmet nor spear flashed on board, and though they shouted through the trumpet all was still. Then Halfred and his followers sprang into the boat, and rowed to the great ship, and saw that it was altogether empty, and climbed on board. And this was the most splendid dragon ship that ever spread sail on the salt seas. But instead of a dragon it bore a silver swan upon the prow.

And moreover also, Halfred told me, the ship was in all things the same as the image he had seen in his night and day dreams; forty oars in iron rowlocks, the deck pavillioned with shields, the sails purple-striped, the prow carved with runes against breakers, and the ropes of sea-dogs' skin. And the high-arched silver wings of the swan were ingeniously carved, and the wind rushed through them with a melodious sound.

And Halfred sprang up to the seat of honour on the upper-deck, upon which lay spread a purple royal mantle, and a silver harp, with a swan's head, leaned against it.

And Halfred said—

> "Singing Swan shalt thou be called, my ship;
> Singing and victorious shalt thou sail."

And many said the elf who had given him his name had sent the Singing Swan to him.

But that is an idle tale of the heathen people. For it has often happened that slightly anchored ships have broken away in storms, while the seamen were carousing ashore.

3

CHAPTER II.

And forthwith it became known that Halfred had armed the best of his house churls, and his followers, with good weapons, to set forth as a Viking to conquer, and as a Skald to sing.

And over the whole of Iceland, and the islands all around, there was much talk about the Singing Swan, which "Oski"[1] himself—that is the god of the heathen people—had sent to Halfred Hamundson. "He is the son of Oski; nothing shall miscarry with him, be it man's hate, or woman's love, in sword thrusts, or in harp playing; great treasure and rich Skald rewards shall he win, and his gentle hand can take and spend, but keep nothing."

And now there came many, drawn to him by the wish to be his sailing comrades, even from the furthest islands of the western sea, so that he could have manned seven ships. He manned, however, only the Singing Swan, with three hundred men whom he chose himself, and with them he set sail upon the sea.

And now there would be much which might be told about the great victories which Halfred won, through many long years, with hammer and harp, on all the seas from Mikilgard—which the Latins call Byzantium—even to the island of Hibernia, in the far west.

And of all these feats and victories, voyages and minstrelsy, and contests of arms and harp playing, had I, as a child by the cloister hearth, heard the Skalds sing, and wandering guests recount, long before I looked into Halfred's sea-grey eyes.

For during the long time that he was wholly lost sight of, and the Singing Swan had vanished in flames, and all people held Halfred for dead, the Skalds composed many songs about him. But that was later.

At that time Halfred thus roamed about everywhere, singing and triumphing, winning fights at sea, and contests in palaces. And because he was victor over all the Skalds in singing competitions, the people named him "Sigskald," and from that, the heathen people, prophesying backwards, invented, perhaps, that fable about the elf which had given him honey, and his name, in the cradle.

And he amassed great spoils, and many hundred rings of red gold, and gave them all away again to his sailing comrades. And yet he still heaped up rich hords upon the Singing Swan; and brought also much treasure to Hamund's hall, where he was wont to pass the winter.

4

And he splendidly improved the hall, and built over against it a great Mead hall, in which a thousand men could drink: and six steps led to the seat of honour in the Mead hall.

But the most costly thing among all his spoils was a candelabrum —"Lampas" the Greeks call it—half as high as a man, of pure gold, with seven flaming arms, which far away, in the land of Greece, he had borne away from a marble city that he had burned.

And this treasure Halfred himself prized highly, who otherwise cared nothing for gold. And at the Yule feast, and the Midsummer feast, and at all high festivals, it must stand close before him upon the table, with its sevenfold flame.

But that at which everyone wondered most was, that all people who saw Halfred, and heard him sing, seemed to be forced to be friendly to him. It often happened that even the Skalds whom he vanquished in song contests, themselves conceived great love for him, and praised his strains more than their own.

But this is truly the most incredible thing that can be told of Skalds. Compared to this it is a small thing that a wooer whom he had supplanted in a woman's favour should become his friend and blood brother. But that was later.

And, indeed, because everything seemed miraculous, those heathen people invented that legend that he was the son of Oski, and that therefore neither men's wrath nor maiden's pride could withstand him; that a god was throned upon his forehead, who dazzled all eyes; with many more such fables.

Above all they say that his smile could conquer all hearts, as the midsummer sun melts the ice.

And about this also they tell a story.

That is, that once, in the depth of winter, he found at the foot of Snaeja-Tjoell, a little maiden of five years old, nearly frozen to death. She had strayed from her mother's cottage, and could not find the way back.

And although Halfred was very weary, and had many followers with him, he sent them all nevertheless alone to the hall, took the child himself upon his shoulder, and travelled many stages further, always tracking the tiny footprints of the little maiden, who had fallen fast asleep, until he found her mother's cottage. And he laid the child in the mother's arms, and she woke and smiled. And the mother wished for him, as a reward, that he should smile henceforth like a child that sees its mother again. And this also had Oski granted to him.

But this is a mere idle tale of the heathen people; for there is no Oski; and no heathen gods; and perchance also no[2] .... I say that he carried the child back himself, carefully, to the mother. Many a Viking would only, from compassion, have thrust her deeper in the snow; the best would have given her to one of his followers to carry to the hall. But to carry her back, himself, through the snow, to her mother, that would no Viking have done that I know; above all when he was tired and hungry.

I say, then, in Halfred there was great goodness of heart, such as is generally wont to be found alone in innocent children; and therefore his smile was heart-winning, as is a child's smile. And out of this, therefore, have the heathen people invented that gift of Oski.

For that he did carry the child to the mother, that I certainly, myself, fully and undoubtingly believe of Halfred. And I would be the last not to believe it of him.

Nevertheless he could become suddenly very wrathful, when the veins in his temples swelled. Then, often, if any enemy roused him by defiance, he would dash, blindly raging, among the spears, like a Berseker.

Over and above all this, they tell many tales of the god-like gifts which made maidens love him. But that is not a miracle, as it comes very near being that a conquered singer should love him.

For he possessed a brilliant noble countenance, which no one forgot who had once seen it, and a heart-winning soft, yet powerful voice. He avoided rude jesting; and he could always divine what was the peculiar charm of every fair maiden's beauty; and he knew how to put it to her as a riddle, over which she herself had long been vainly pondering.

But other riddles, also, he knew well how to find out.

CHAPTER III.

And thus had Halfred now, for many years, roamed about as a Viking and as a Skald, and had won fame and red gold; and once more he again celebrated the Yule feast at home in his hall.

And there were very many hundred men assembled there in the Mead hall which he had fitted up. All his sailing comrades, and very many Icelanders, and many foreign guests, from Austrvegr, and even from Hylmreck, and Dyflin, on the western sea. Among them also the Skald, Vandrad, from Tiunderland.

And the Bragi cup[3] passed round, and many men vowed vows thereon, and many a one pledged himself to daring deeds, which he would perform before Midsummertide, or die. Halfred also, as well as the guests, had drunk a great deal of mead; more than he was wont to drink, as he himself, afterwards, earnestly told me.

And this also the heathen point to in him as a miraculous gift of his father Oski; that he could drink far far more than other men, in fact—and they hold him therein very lucky—as many horns full as he chose, without the heron of forgetfulness[4] sweeping through his dizzied brain.

But this is foolishly said, for even I can scare away the heron, if I, after each draught, think quietly to myself, and do not propose many toasts; for such attract the heron.

Halfred had now certainly emptied many horns; but as yet he had vowed no vow. Silent and grave he sat in the seat of the honour, as befitted the host; exhorted the tardy drinkers—there were not however many of them—by sending the cup bearer to them, with the drinking horn; and smiled quietly, when many a one vowed vows which he would never fulfil.

Then arose from his seat Vandrad the Skald, from Tiunderland, and stood upon the second step of the dais, and spoke. Halfred had vanquished him five times, and yet the Skald was a faithful loving friend to him—

> "Vows have here been now vowed by many
> Guests of small worth.
> But Halfred, the Lord of the mead hall,
> Still holds his thoughts hidden.
> I laud him, most lofty,
> No vows hath he need of,
> His name may content him.
> Yet I miss in the mead hall
> One thing to the mighty,

To the man is awanting
A maiden to wife.
What rapture if only,
From the high seat of honour,
The horn to us, downward,
The dazzling white hand
Of the nobly born Princess,
Harthild, should hold."

All the guests kept silence when Vandrad had spoken. Halfred looked proudly down upon him, and very gently, he told me later, he felt the veins in his temples swell, as, smiling, he asked the Skald—but it was the smile of a king, not a child's smile—

"And what then of Harthild,
Her beauty and fame,
Canst thou here sound the praise,
In Halfred's mead hall?"

Then said Vandrad—

"For all that thou knowest,
Thou far roaming Viking,
Hast thou never heard Harthild's
Descent and renown
Proclaimed on the harp?
From Upsala's ancient
Deep rooted stem
The maiden is sprung.
Hartstein the Haggard,
Men call her father,
The powerful monarch
Of far spreading fame.
His daughter close guarded
He haughtily holds;
All wooers rejecting,
Who cannot excel him
In throwing the hammer.
And no less the maiden
All men avoideth,
Man-like her own mood.
With good cause she boasteth
Herself in deep riddles
Above all the Skalds
Skilful to be.
'Breaker of men's wits'
In dread and in envy,
They call her in Nordland.
To every wooer
Who fain her proud spirit
In wedlock would bind,
Tells she the same
Close sealed riddle;
For none—not the wisest—
Has ever yet solved it.
Then scornfully laughing,
With her sharp scissors,

> —For so runs the statute—
> To shame him, she sheareth
> From the hero his hair."

Then Halfred's temple veins swelled fearfully. He shook back the thick black locks which flowed down even to his shoulders, and drained off a deep drinking horn. Then he sprang from his seat, and seized the Bragi cup, on which vows were wont to be vowed. Once more he paused, set down the Bragi cup again, and asked—

> "But Skald, say now, quickly,
> —Oft hast thou seen her—
> This men avoider.
> Beautiful is she?
> This breaker of men's wits,
> Would the bride's wreath become her?"

Vandrad replied—

> "Nor soft nor gentle,
> Is she, nor lovely,
> But proud and stately
> Stands her tall form.
> Nor could another
> Carry so fitly
> The crown of a king."

Then Halfred again took up the Bragi cup, strode forward to the highest step which led to his seat of honour, and paused where exactly in the centre was burned into the oaken floor a circle, in red runes, so small that a man could only tread therein with one foot. Halfred kneeled down, planted his left foot within the circle, and lifted the Bragi cup in his right hand, high above his head.

And all were very eager to hear what he would now say; for this was the strongest, the most solemn form in which vow could be vowed. And Halfred said—

> "Ere yet the on coming
> Midsummer tide
> Shall sink in the sea,
> Will I bring Harthild,
> The daughter of Hartstein,
> Here as my wife,
> To dwell in my hall,
> Or hold me shall Hell.

> "Her wit-breaking sayings
> Will I lay bare,
> Her runic riddles
> Will I unfold.
> Unshamed, and unshaven,
> These black locks shake freely.
> Her man-despising
> Maiden mood quelling,

9

My wedded wife
Will force her to be.
The breaker of men's wits
Will I break in.
A right noble heir
Of all that I own
She shall here, in my hall,
Soon cherish, my son.
And softly shall sing him
To sleep with the songs
Of his father's great deeds,
Or hold me shall Hell."

Thus ended the Yule feast, at that time; for all the guests started up from their seats with a great uproar, in a confused throng, and drank to Halfred, and shouted that this was the best and most admirable vow which in the memory of man had been vowed in the north.

And the tumult was so great that Halfred had to command silence from the dais, and very soon to send round the parting cup to the uproarious heroes.

And Halfred told me that when, under the light of the stars, he crossed the court to his dwelling-house, he repented of his vow. Not because he feared King Hartstein's hammer-throwing, or dreaded his daughter's riddle. But because it is always wiser for a man to see a maiden, before he determines to make her his wife.

CHAPTER IV.

And so soon as the Austr-Vogen was free from ice, the Singing Swan sailed towards Svearike, and through numberless perils into the great sea which lies to the south and east of Upland; and from thence she followed a river, as far as there was floating depth, upwards towards Tiunderland, and to Upsala.

And many will now believe that Halfred had a great struggle and much difficulty to overcome King Hartstein and his daughter, and will expect to hear how it came to pass.

But there is nothing to tell; for everything went easily and quickly with him, according to his wishes, which the heathen people again boasted had been thus arranged by Oski.

King Hartstein was, in general, a flinty-hearted man, full of suspicion, and short of speech. When, however, he saw Halfred, and called to him as he entered his hall, and drew near to the throne, and asked him—"Stranger, what desirest thou in Tiunderland, and of King Hartstein?"—And when Halfred, with that smile which Oski had bestowed upon him, looked into the fierce eyes, and joyously replied—"The best will I have that Tiunderland and King Hartstein possess—his daughter." Then the grim old man was at once won, and in his secret heart he wished that Halfred might be his son-in-law.

And then they went out to the court for the hammer-throwing, and the King threw well, but Halfred threw far better, and thus the first trial was won.

"Harder will thou find the second," said the old man, and led Halfred to the Skemma, the chamber of the women, where the breaker of men's wits, in a shining dark blue mantle, sat among her maidens, a head taller than any of them.

And they say that when Halfred entered the chamber, and his glance fell upon her, a hot tremor passed over her, and a sudden glow dyed her cheeks crimson, and confused her.

Certain it is that with a golden spindle, with which she had played rather than spun, she pricked her finger, and let it fall with a clatter.

But Sudha, the foremost of her maidens, the captive daughter of the King of Halogaland, who sat at her right hand, picked up the spindle, and held it. And many interpreted this later, as a bad omen. At the time, however, it was hardly observed.

And Vandrad the Skald said later to Halfred, that the woman had been elf-struck at the first sight of him: but he thereupon said earnestly—"It had been better had I been elf-struck at sight of her; but I remained unwounded."

And forthwith King Hartstein assembled all his courtiers, and the women of the castle, and the guests, in the hall, for the riddle solving.

And Harthild arose from the arm chair at his right hand, and her face grew crimson as she looked at Halfred, which—as they declare—had never before happened to her at the challenging of her riddle.

She paused for a space, looked downwards, then again upon Halfred, and now with searching and defiant eyes. And she began—

> "What is held in Valhalla?
> What is hidden in Hell?
> What hammers in hammer?
> And heads the strong helm?
> What begins the host slaughter?
> What closes a sigh?
> And what holds in Harthild
> The head and the heart?"

Then she would have seated herself, as was her wont after giving out the riddle; but struck by terror she remained standing, and grasped the arm of the chair; for Halfred, without any reflecting, stretched his right hand towards her, and spoke—

> "Hast thou nothing harder,
> Haughty one, hidden?
> Then wreathe thy proud head
> For Hymen in haste,
> For what's held in Valhalla,
> What's hidden in Hell,
> What hammers in hammer,
> And heads the strong helm,
> What begins the host slaughter,
> And closes a sigh,
> What Harthild the haughty
> The head and the heart holds,
> What hovers deep hidden
> In high thoughts of her heart,
> And what here has Halfred
> To proud Harthild holpen,
> 'Tis the Sacred Rune
> The hero's own H."

Then Harthild sank pale with rage in her chair, and covered her head with her veil.

But when Hartstein, her father, drew near amidst loud cries of astonishment from the listeners in the hall, and would have drawn the veil from her face, she sprang up vehemently, threw back the veil—and they saw that she had wept—and cried in a harsh voice—

"Well has thou solved
The hidden riddle.
With mighty wit
Hast won a wife,
Woe to thee if tenderly
Thou usest her not!"

All kept silence, uneasy at these threatening unloving words. Halfred at length broke the stillness, he threw back his head, and shook his black locks, and laughed—"I will risk that! King Hartstein, this very day will I pay thee the bride's dower. When prepare we the bridal feast?"

CHAPTER V.

King Hartstein, however, wished for delay, until Hartvik and Eigil should have returned from a campaign. Then their reception feast and the marriage could be celebrated together.

Hartvik was the king's son, and Harthild's own brother; and Eigil was son to the king's brother, and Harthild's cousin.

And he would willingly have taken Harthild away as his wife, but she had said to him, "If thou failest to solve my riddle, thy shorn locks will cause thee affliction; and if thou solvest my riddle, and I become thy wife, that will cause thee still deeper affliction, for no love for thee dwells in my heart: and woe to him who without love wins me for his wife."

Then Eigil sadly gave it up, although he was a good riddle solver.

And when Hartvik and Eigil were returned there soon grew to be a great friendship between Halfred and Hartvik, and Halfred and Eigil, and both loved him so well that they said they would lay down their lives for him.

And this between Halfred and Hartvik is no great wonder, because Halfred always won all men's hearts.

But it may well astonish many that Eigil also should thus love him, who still cherished as much love to Harthild as formerly; and who yet clearly saw, as all who had eyes could see, that the harsh maiden was quite filled with love to Halfred.

And jealousy does not often allow it to be admitted that the nightingale has a more charming voice than the carrion crow.

Hartvik and Egil, however, loved Halfred so dearly that they begged him to receive them as his blood brothers.

And on the day before the wedding feast was prepared, therefore, Hartvik and Eigil became Halfred's blood brethren.

They stood with him, as the heathen people do, under a strip of turf, which was lifted on spear points above their heads, the two ends still cleaving to the ground, and they mixed the blood which flowed from gashes in their right arms down upon the black earth beneath their feet.

And therewith they vowed their heads for ever to the infernal gods if ever one of the blood brothers should desert the other, in danger or in need. And so strongly does this oath bind, that even against his own kith and kin, yea even

14

against his own father, must one blood brother stand by the other, even until death.

CHAPTER VI.

On the day after the wedding, however, Halfred rode alone into the pine wood. He said he wished to think, and he refused Harthild, who would have ridden with him, and also his blood brethren.

Darkly Harthild looked after him as he rode out of the court. But Sudha, the beautiful daughter of the King of Halogaland, also looked after him from an overhanging window, and slowly stroked her blue black hair back from her temples.

Vandrad the Skald, however, who often staid at Hartstein's Court, and who was there at that time, had long cherished love for Sudha. And he had often begged her freedom from King Hartstein, but in vain; the stern man had always denied him.

And heretofore she had not listened unwillingly when he sang. But when in these days he drew near to her, and spoke of a song which he had composed in her praise, she turned away and said—"On the lips of one only have the gods laid honey."

And when in the evening Halfred returned from the pinewood towards the royal castle, he was leading his weary horse by the bridle, for the moon shone but fitfully through storm-rent clouds, there sat upon the runic-stone hard by the road a closely veiled woman, and she cried to him and said—

"Halfred Hamundson, whereof on the first day of thy marriage, ridest thou alone in the pinewood?"

"If thou knowest that, O wise Vala," said Halfred, pausing—and he heaved a sigh—"then knowest thou more than Halfred Hamundson."

"I will tell thee," replied the veiled one. "Thou hast sought a woman, and found what is nigher to a man, rough, harsh, and devoid of charm. The Singing Swan hath paired thee with the vulture's brood. Thou chosest the hard flint stone, near to it lay glowing at thy feet the rose, exhaling fragrance towards thee."

Then Halfred sprang upon his horse, and cried to the veiled one—

"Nobler hold I it in a woman to be too cold, than too ardent." And he dashed away.

And only once, as he told me, he looked back. So beautiful, he said, had she never before been, in the full light of day, as now in the moonlight, her black eyes glittered—for she had torn off her head covering—and she called after him by his name, "Halfred," and her blue-black hair fluttered round her in the night wind like a ghostly veil.

CHAPTER VII.

And when the depth of winter was passed, and the spring was come, Halfred sent a message to Upsala, to King Hartstein, that at the midsummer tide Dame Harthild should bear a child.

And the wise women had thrown runic rods over her seven times, and had learned each time by unerring signs that the child should be a son. And already was his name chosen, "Sigurd Sigskaldson."

And Halfred bade the king, and Hartvik and Eigil, and Vandred the Skald, and all the people from the castle at Upsala, as many as the ships would hold, to be his guests at Hamund's hall, twenty nights before the midsummer tide.

And there, at the birth and naming of the boy, a great feast should be held, such as had never before been held in Iceland.

And King Hartstein gave answer that he and all his people, as many as twelve ships could carry, would come as bidden, to the feast.

Thus at the beginning of the month of roses came King Hartstein, and Hartvik, and Eigil, and many hundred men from the castle at Upsala; and people from all parts of Tiunderland.

And among the women who came also, the first that descended from the ship was Sudha. She had begged that she might come, out of longing to see Harthild.

And again there was close friendship between Halfred and his blood-brethren, Hartvik and Eigil. They shared their table and bread and salt.

Thus they waited the birth of the heir of the hall, on the midsummer day, and made ready a great feast in the Mead hall.

Rich hangings of silken and woven stuffs which Halfred had borne away from the islands of Greece were spread upon the wooden walls of the drinking hall; the floor was strewn deep with rushes and clean straw, and the tables and benches were set out in two long rows, and one cross row.

On all the pillars of the walls were hung curiously interlaced weapons, which the Viking had gathered from boarded ships, stormed castles, and victorious battlefields. But on sideboards around were set out the many cups and horns of gold, silver, bronze, amber, and precious horn, which the Sigskald had won, by singing in the halls of kings.

But straight before Halfred towered the lofty candalabrum from Greece, with its seven flaming arms.

Eigil and Hartvik were to sit on his left hand, the guests from Tiunderland and the other strangers on the long benches to the right, the house churls and islanders on the long benches to the left of the dais. And the most honoured guests had even cushions for the back, brought from a pillared marble house which had been burnt on the coast of Rumaberg.

The women, however, were not to come into the hall, but to tarry with Harthild, and await her hour in the chamber of the women.

This was all splendidly ordered, and Halfred himself told me that never, neither as guest nor as host, had he seen such magnificent festival preparations.

Two days before the feast, as Halfred, wearied with the summer heat, lay upon his couch after the mid-day meal, Sudha glided softly through the doorway, and stood before him, and spoke—

"Halfred, skill in song, victory and fame have been thine for twenty years.

A wife hast thou had for one year—an heir shalt thou have but now.

But never hast thou known Freya's gift—Love's Fulness—

Contradict me not—thine eye shuns Dame Harthild's seeking glance;

And when thou dreamingly sweepest the strings of thy harp, thou gazest

Not in Dame Harthild's cold hard face, but upwards towards the stars.

Halfred, not in the clouds dwelleth that for which thou yearnest.

Not from the stars shall it float down upon thee; upon the earth it wanders,

It is a woman, who with love's charm, with woman's magic, can subdue the Singing Swan—

Woe to thee if thou never findest her—

What though thou win all fame with sword and harp—the best is still denied thee.

Askest thou what maketh me so wise, and withal so daring?

Love, love's fulness for thee, thou rich yet poor Sigskald.

Behold, I am but a woman—a captive—but I tell thee there is heroism even for women.

I have sworn by the infernal gods, as I crossed thy threshold, that here, in Iceland, I will win thy love, or die."

Then Halfred arose from his couch, and spoke—

"Wisdom and madness mingled hast thou spoken. There speaks from thee more than Sudha. There speaks a soul stricken of the gods.

Horror and compassion seize upon me. I will demand thy freedom from King Hartstein. Then journey homewards to Halagoland.

There mayest thou find happiness in the arms of some valiant hero.

But here, let Dame Harthild's rights and hearth be sacred unto thee. Disturb not her happiness."

And he seized his spear and strode out. But Sudha cried after him, so that he still heard her—"Her happiness? Long has she divined her misery. Soon shall she clearly perceive, the haughty one, that she is more unspeakably wretched than Sudha."

Then, the evening of the same day, she called to her Vandrad the Skald, who still always cherished great love for her, to the well in the court, as though she would beg him to draw up for her from the depth the heavy water bucket. This did Vandrad later, when dying, himself tell Halfred.

But when he had raised the bucket to the edge of the well, she lightly laid a finger on his bare arm, and said—

"Vandrad, come hither to-night, just when the star Oervandil is mirrored in this well. Thou shall tell me all that formerly came to pass here, about that oath on the Bragi cup."

Vandrad considered within himself, and he looked doubtingly at her.

Then she said—"Vandrad, I swear to thee by ⁵Freya's throat jewels that I will become thy wife when I leave this island. Wilt thou now come and tell me all?"

Then Vandrad swore to do what she required.

CHAPTER VIII.

And now the midsummer feast was magnificently celebrated in the hall. And there were full a thousand guests within the hall; but many hundreds of the servants and bondmen were camped round about the building, in the open air.

Besides the guests from Svearike, there had come from all the neighbouring coasts and islands many jarl's and great chieftains. Thus from distant Iceland, the kings Konal, and Kiartan from Dyflin; from Zealand the Danish Jarl Hako, and Sveno from Lethra; then from West Gothaland the three brothers, Arnbiorn, Arngeir, and Arnolfr; Jarls of the Western Goths. There had long been a blood feud, which had been but newly allayed with blood money, between these three, and the two brothers Princes of East Gothaland, Helge and Helgrimr.

And these two, and the other three, would only come with a strong well-armed following, when they understood that their adversaries had also been bidden to Halfred's feast.

And Halfred had taken care that the followers of the Princes of West Gothaland should be lodged to the right, and those of East Gothaland to the left, at the back of the hall, in huts of pinewood. And a wooden wall with strongly closed doors divided the two encampments.

But also from other vallies of Svearik, besides Tiunderland, from Tronland, from Herjadel, Jeutland, and Helsingaland, had come many guests, who had often of old been enemies to the people from Tiunderland.

The feast, however, proceeded most joyously from daybreak even until the night. And when within the hall, and without, where the foreign servants were encamped, many fires and pine torches were kindled—before Halfred burned the seven armed candelabrum—it was at first a right jovial sun fire-feast.

The men, swinging and emptying the drinking horns, sprang over the flames, and the Skalds, in songs which they composed at the moment they rose, vied with each other in praises of Halfred and his deeds with hammer and harp, and of the Singing Swan, and the hall, and the feast.

And all the foreign kings also proclaimed that never had they seen so lordly a midsummer feast celebrated, neither at home, nor in the halls of any other host.

Halfred sat with a joyful heart in the seat of honour. He signed to his harp-bearer to bring him his silver harp, for he wished at the last, to requite the laudations of the Skalds and the praises of the guests with thanks and a song of welcome…. And then began that catastrophe which was to overwhelm Halfred and his house, and the men of Tiunderland, and all the guests, and many other men and women, altogether strange and far away, who had never even seen or heard of Halfred and Harthild, in blood and fire.

That is to say, the great door of the hall, exactly opposite to the seat of honour opened, and Dame Harthild strode in.

Haughtily erect she walked, her head thrown back. A long black mantle was wrapped around her head and neck and breast, and her whole body; it floated trailing after her, like the curling wave behind a ship's stern.

And Halfred said to one it seemed to him, then, as if the most fearful of the Fates was striding through the hall.

Straight up the hall she passed, followed by Sudha and her women, her glance fixed upon Halfred.

Slowly, silently, she ascended the six steps of the dais, and paused straight before Halfred at the table. Only the heavy candelabrum stood between the two.

But all the men in the hall sat speechless, and gazed up at the black woman, who looked like a dark thunder cloud.

"Halfred Hamundson," she began—and her voice was loud, yet toneless —"Answers I demand to two questions, before these ten hundred hearers in thy hall. Lie not to me."

The blood rose to Halfred's brow, and he felt his temple veins throb heavily. "If I speak or act," he said to himself, "I know neither what I should say nor do. Therefore I will keep silence and do nothing."

But Harthild, with her left hand pressed upon her thigh, continued—"Didst thou, in that first night, when I held thy hand firm upon my girdle, and asked thee if thou lovedst me, say Yes or No? Answer me Sigskald. I and the gods know about that."

"Yes," said Halfred, and knitted his brows.

"And is it true, as Vandrad the Skald has sworn, that here, in this hall, at the Yule feast, after many horns of mead, thou didst vow, as a wanton wager, that before the midsummer tide, thou would break in the breaker of men's wits like a stubborn horse, and that to make good these boasting words thou camest to Tiunderland, and remained, as thou didst lament, unwounded at sight of me."

"Speak the truth—lie not again—a thousand listeners hear thee—thou lordly son of Oski—Is it so?"

Then Halfred raged in his inmost heart, but he constrained himself, and replied firmly and distinctly—

"It is as thou hast said."

Then Harthild drew herself up yet higher, and like two serpents flashed, glances of fearful hatred from her eyes, as she spoke—

"So be thou accursed, from the crown of thy head to the sole of thy foot, thou who hast deceived and
    disgraced a hapless woman;

Cursed be thy proud thoughts—Madness shall strike them;

Cursed be thy false eyes—Blindness shall smite them;

Cursed be thy lying lips—They shall wither and smile no more;

Cursed be thy flattering voice—It shall be dumb;

Thy house and thy hall shall perish in flames—The Singing Swan shall burn;

Thy hand shall be crippled—thy hammer not strike—thy harp shall shatter;

Victory shall be denied thee in battle and in song;

Nothing shall any more delight thee, in which of yore thou hast rejoiced;

The sun of spring—the flowers of the forest—the fire of wine—the blackbird's song—the greeting of
    the evening star—Sleepless shall roll thy groaning head, and if slumber draws near to thee it
    shall be with stifling dreams.

Yet a twofold curse shall rend ye both, if thou winnest again a woman's love.

In madness and disease shall she perish whom thou lovest more than thy soul.

But the son whom I, wretched one, must bear, shall be his mother's avenger upon his father.

Liar's son, Scoundrel's son, Harthild's Vengeance shall his name be.

And one day, villain, shall he smite thee, as here, to shame thee before all men, my hand now strikes
    thee in the face."

And she lifted high her outspread right hand, and aimed a blow over the
table at Halfred's head.

Halfred sprang up, and to avert such a disgrace threw up his left arm. Then
he struck the heavy seven flaming candalabrum; with a crash the metal fell
with all its flaming arms upon Dame Harthild's breast and body, and then
upon the ground.

As though struck by lightning stood the woman all in flames—mantle and
hair blazed up. At once the fire caught the straw thickly strewn upon the floor.

"King Hartstein, avenge thy unhappy child," shrieked Harthild, in agony.
She believed that in rage Halfred had hurled the candalabrum upon her.

The king believed the same, and whilst Halfred grasped at the blazing
woman to rescue her, Kling Hartstein with a cry of "Down thou scoundrel,"
struck him a sharp sword stroke on the forehead, so that he fell stunned.

And with a second blow he would have slain him, had not Eigil and
Hartvik sprung up and quickly borne away their blood brother.

Thus it came to pass that from the very outset Halfred could neither avert
nor control this catastrophe—He alone could have done it.

Now, however, the burning woman and the flaming straw filled everyone
with sudden frenzy.

24

The people from Tiunderland rose up in fury when they saw their king's daughter fall flaming on the crackling straw; and Halfred's comrades drew their swords when they saw their lord fall bleeding. And flame and smoke, shrieks of women, and avenging shouts of men filled the hall.

Then broke loose a fighting and devastation in the hall so gigantic, say the heathen people, that the like shall never be seen again until the twilight of the gods, when all demons and giants, goblins and elves, gnomes, menkind, and pigmies, shall slay each other, and heaven, earth and hell shall perish in flames.

Harthild in her burning clothes, was carried out by her shrieking women. One only was missing. Sudha sprang through flames and arms to where Halfred lay on his blood-brethren's knees.

"Dead," she cried; "Slain by Sudha. Then share we death, if not life." And she drew Halfred's dagger from his belt, and plunged it in her own breast.

"Slain Halfred! by my babbling tongue. Sudha slain!" cried Vandrad the Skald. "I will avenge thee, Halfred."

And he tore a casting spear from the trophies hanging on the flame-wreathed wooden pillars, and hurled it whistling at the temples of King Hartstein, so that he fell dead.

Wildly shouted the people of Tiunderland, and their near kindred from West Gothaland, for vengeance for Harthild and King Hartstein.

And the Jarl Ambiorn, from West Gothaland, seized in both hands a heavy brazen double-handled tankard, and dashed it down on Vandrad's forehead, so that he fell.

But when the Princes from East Gothaland saw this, that their mortal foes aided the men from Upsala, then they fell, Helgi and Helgrimr, with furious blows upon both their old enemies, and the guests from Upsala.

And now could none any longer give a thought to extinguishing the blazing straw upon the floor, or the quickly burning silken and woollen hangings on the walls or the wooden pillars, up which tongues of flame were creeping.

For blindly now flew spears and axes, and golden and silver drinking horns; and many who would have striven for peace, or trodden out the flames, had fallen, struck down by both sides.

"Must we alone stand idle among the strange guests at this bloody midsummer feast?" said the Danish Jarl Hako, to the Irish King Konal, "so that the Skalds shall taunt us as drink valiant but battle shy. We have an old strife about stolen horses. Let us fight it out here, thou Irish Greenpeak!"

"Thou drunkard of Zealand," was the answer, "I will quench for ever thy thirst and thy reviling;" and he struck his broad short Irish knife through his teeth into his throat.

Then Sveno, his brother, fell furiously upon the Irish king, and their followers, Danes and Irish, fought by themselves their own battle in the forefront of the hall, and thus blocked up the door, so that no one could escape from the hall into the open air.

And those who had no weapons tore down the trophies from the pillars, or hurled about the heavy drinking horns, and even the flaming beams and blocks which already fell from the ceiling, and instead of shields they defended themselves with the tables.

And all wildly mingled fought the people of Tiunderland and Iceland, of Westgothaland and Eastgothaland, of Zealand and Ireland. And hardly did anyone know who was friend or foe; and many, many men sank down, wounded or burnt.

And at last the flames had burst through the roof, and shot blazing up towards heaven.

And as the wind from above blew down upon the swelling hangings on the walls, they flashed up suddenly in a brighter blaze.

And now the highest beam fell with a crash; and thereupon rang out a sound as though forty harp strings had all at once uttered their dying wail. And it was even so, for the beam had severed in twain Halfred's silver harp, which lay close by his head.

At this wailing harp cry Halfred opened his eyes, and looked around him, and all the truth broke upon him. He sprang up and shouted threateningly through slaughter and flames—Hartvik and Eigil protected him with shield and sword—

"Hold! Peace, peace in the hall! Magic has frenzied us all! Quench, quench the fire which devours us all!"

And so great was his power over friends and foes that for a moment all paused.

Then hark! From without there thundered on the hindmost door of the hall heavy axe strokes, and the cry—

"Halfred, Halfred, save thy house! Save the Singing Swan!"

With a crash the door fell inwards, and new devastation was seen, which kindled afresh the momentarily smothered battle fury in the hall.

Halfred looked through the doorway. The house of his forefathers, and the ships in the harbour, and the Singing Swan were all wrapped in flames.

The followers of the princes of Westgothaland, who were lodged in the pine huts, had first heard the din of battle, and seen the flames in the hall. "To the rescue—to the rescue of our lords," they shouted, tore down the wooden wall that divided them from the Mead hall, and hurried to their aid.

But then there threw themselves upon them, to hinder them, their hostile neighbours, the followers of the princes of Eastgothaland, who being too weak to hold the open field, retreated partly into Halfred's dwelling house, partly to their ships in the Fjord.

With shouts of triumph the victors followed, crowded with the fugitives into Halfred's dwelling house, and stormed the ships in the bay; and dwelling house and ships were suddenly wrapped in flames, either set on fire by the combatants, or ignited by sparks and burning splinters, borne by the strong south wind from the roof of the Mead hall.

Halfred threw one glance at his shattered harp, and the burning house of his fathers; then he grasped his hammer firmer, and cried—

"Come hither to me all Halfred's comrades. Quit the hall. Save the Swan!"

And with a mighty onslaught, swinging his hammer round his head, he burst through the ranks of the men who had already renewed the battle in the hall.

Hartvik and Eigil followed on his track, and many of his own people, and also of the enemy.

But those who did not leave the drinking hall with him were almost all at once numbered with the dead. For with a heavy crash, close behind Halfred, fell the whole burning roof into the hall.

Halfred glanced back in his rapid course. High upwards shot the blaze, mingling with sound of shrieks from hundreds slain. Then all was silent in the midsummer feast hall.

Halfred rushed on, followed by friends and foes, past his father's house. He saw the flames creeping up the pillars; within rose the din of raging conflict; on the threshold lay a slaughtered servant girl.

Soon Halfred and his comrades reached the bay, where the battle surged around the high-decked ships. Many were burning. Many dragon's heads seemed to vomit fire and smoke.

Around the Singing Swan, however, raged the battle most furiously. In dense masses the enemy thronged round her, wading, swimming, in boats and on rafts, they crowded on; others hurled spears and arrows from the shore at her defenders, and more than one burning arrow had struck and set fire to her.

The left wing of the ingeniously carved Swan was on fire; tongues of fire were creeping up ropes and sails—just as Halfred arrived they caught the mast.

Then grief and fury seized upon him. His temple veins swelled almost to the size of a child's finger.

"Quench, quench the flames! All hands on deck! Save the Swan! Cut the anchor-cable. Put out to sea. Fight no more. I will fight for you all."

His faithful followers obeyed him. The seamen left off fighting, and laboured only to quench the flames, in which also they soon succeeded, as no more arrows flew from the land, and the foe were forced to leave the ship.

For Halfred raged furiously, as none had ever seen him fight. With a loud battle-cry he sprang upon the people of Westgothaland and Tiunderland, and struck them down one after another.

Loyally aided him Hartvik and Eigil, his blood brethren, and spared not even their own countrymen and kindred; but thought rather on the blood oath which bound them more closely to Halfred than to their own kinsmen.

And the foe fell back before Halfred and his comrades, from the open field into the dwelling house, which was half burned down, and barricaded it.

And thus he stormed his own house, in which the people from Westgothaland had before overcome the house churls and the East Goths, and slain them all.

Yet a whole hour lasted the conflict. There Halfred, on the threshold of his house, slew the Danish Jarl Sveno, the last chieftain of the enemy who still lived, and pressed into the house with his men.

The people from Westgothaland, Zealand, and Tiunderland, defended themselves like bears at bay. But at last they were all slain. And from thence Halfred returned to the Mead hall, which was still glowing, and searched who there still lived.

But there, also, all were dead.

And they found the bodies of King Hartstein, and Sudha, and of the Dane Hako, and the two Irishmen, Konal and Kiartan, of the Eastgothic Prince Helge—Helgrimr had fallen on board ship—and of Arngeir and Arnbiorn— Arnolfr had been slain in the dwelling house—and they found Vandrad the

Skald at the point of death.

Then he told Halfred how Sudha had prevailed upon him to speak, and begged him to forgive him the death of so many heroes. And Halfred held his hand until he was dead.

But Dame Harthild's body they did not find, although many of her women lay burnt or slain in the dwelling-house.

But many bodies were so burnt and charred they could not be recognised.

And then they turned their search to the ships.

And all the ships of the foreign guests were burnt, and all those of the Icelanders which lay in the bay. For at the last, by reason of Halfred's furious attack, no one had thought any more about extinguishing them.

And Halfred, with his trumpet, hailed the Singing Swan, which floated saved in the moonlight, and went on board with his little troop.

And there lay slain many hundreds of Halfred's Icelanders,

The foreign guests, however, who had come to the midsummer feast, lay all all dead, save only Hartvik and Eigil.

And Halfred counted when he called all hands before the mast still seventy men alive.

All the rest had fallen in that one midsummer night. And there fell after that wild tumult an awful stillness upon land and sea. And sad and silent floated the Singing Swan, with scorched sails, upon the Fjord.

CHAPTER IX.

And Halfred has sunk into deep deep silence. Since the fight had ended, and he had heard Vandrad's dying words, he had not spoken a word.

But when it was full daylight the Singing Swan drew near the land, and the men came ashore.

Silently Halfred signed to his sailing comrades to carry out all the bodies from the drinking hall, the dwelling-house, and the ships; and to collect them altogether on the shore. He had seven funeral piles erected, and upon these all the dead were burned with their weapons. The ashes, however, of friends and foes Halfred ordered them to mingle.

And these he poured himself into a great stone-lined grave which he had had dug on the shore, hard by the water line. And he had earth heaped thickly upon them, and a huge black block of stone which had once been thrown out of Hekla rolled thereon. And this cost many days work.

But Halfred spoke not. And all through the nights he sat upon the grave and looked now upwards to the stars of the summer night, now downwards rigidly upon the earth, and the stone grave. And gently gently he oftimes shook his head.

But he spoke no word.

And when after seven nights the sun arose, Hartvik and Eigil drew near to him, as he sat upon the stone, and then Hartvik spoke—

"Halfred, my blood brother, a great calamity has befallen to thee, to me, to us. Father and sister and many friends have I lost, and Eigil has also lost many who were dear to him. We must bear it, all three. Come, Halfred, Sigskald, arouse thyself! This silence and brooding is evil. Dwelling-house and Mead hall the fire has burnt—the axe will build them up. Harps, there are many still upon the earth, and the Singing Swan spreads out her hardly singed pinions. Come, Halfred, drink! Here I have brought thee from the Greek spoils of the Singing Swan a cup of Chios wine, which thou ever lovedst. Drink, speak, and live!"

Halfred stood up with a sigh, took the cup from Hartvik's hand, and poured the wine slowly upon the grave; the earth drank it greedily in.

"Come hither again about midnight. Then will I give ye an answer. I cannot even yet think clearly. Once more will I ask the gods who dwell in the stars if they even yet deny me an answer."

And he sat down again upon the stone, and covered his face with his hands.

And when about midnight the two came, Halfred pointed towards the heavens—

"There are so many thousand thousand stars, but they are all dumb to me.

Unceasingly, for seven days and nights, have I asked myself, and asked the stars, wherefore have the Gods allowed this awful thing to happen?

Is it a crime that I vowed a vow, such as many which are vowed in the north?

Hundreds of women had heard it without resentment.

Is it my crime that Dame Harthild was differently minded?

And it was no lie that I bore love to her, on that night.

Love's fulness truly it was not—as Sudha named it.

That may be. Never knew I love's fulness.

And be it so. If the Gods hate me for an evil deed, wherefore do they not punish me alone?

Wherefore let others—so many others—suffer and atone for *my* sin?

Wherefore should King Hartstein perish, and many other princes, and thousands of men from all coasts and islands?

Wherefore should Dame Harthild perish, whom they would have avenged, and our unborn son?

How have all these sinned? Answer me, ye two, if ye know more than do I and the stars?"

But his blood brethren were silent, and Halfred continued—

"Yet there must be Gods!

Who has else bound the giants, calmed the sea, levelled the earth, arched the heavens, and strewn the stars? Who else guides the battle? and how, after death, come mighty heroes to Valhalla, and the evil to the dark serpent hell?

For that awful fearful thought which already from afar has come darkly into my mind, that perhaps no Gods live! I will think it no more.

There must be Gods. I cannot cannot think otherwise, and my throbbing brain is driven to frenzy.

And if there are Gods, they must be also good, and wise, and mighty, and just.

Else it would be indeed yet more frightful to think that beings, mightier and wiser than mankind, delighted in the misery of men, like an evil urchin who for sport impales a captured beetle.

This, therefore, one dare not think,—neither, indeed,—that there are no Gods, or that there are evil Gods.

And therefore will I in devout submission endure this awful calamity, waiting till, in the course of years, I guess this riddle also. So hard an one was never yet set before me.

But ye, ye faithful ones, who stood by me to the death, and spared not your own kindred, and have lost your nearest through me; ye will I never forsake, all my life long; and great gratitude will I bear ye, and my dearest shall ye be for evermore. For ye alone will I live."

Then spake Hartvik—

"Not thus must thou speak, Halfred. The harp thou shalt again strike victoriously, the hammer shalt thou again joyously wield under the blue heavens of Greece. The blood of the vine shalt thou quaff, and a woman more enchanting than—"

Then Halfred sprang up from the black stone—

"Silence, Hartvik: Thou blasphemest.

Who is stricken so heavily as I, by the hatred of the Gods, who live and are just, he stands as a lightning-blasted tree by the way. Birds sing not upon it, the dew moistens it not, the sun kisses it not.

How should I sing and laugh, drink and kiss, through whom hath fallen upon so many thousand men and women utter destruction, or the sorrow of death for evermore?

No, otherwise have I vowed to myself.

Long did I doubt if I still could live, after such a calamity as the Gods have laid upon this head, and I could not, did I not believe in good Gods, and tarry for the solving of this riddle.

But joy and happiness have no more part in Halfred Hamundson. I renounce them for ever."

And he kneeled down, and took from his breast pouch a leathern bottle, which was filled with white ashes. And slowly he strewed them all over his long flowing black locks, and his face, and breast, and body.

"Hear me, ye good all ruling Gods, and ye glittering all seeing stars of heaven; and of men-kind upon earth, Hartvik and Eigil, my blood brethren!

Here I renounce, on account of the awful calamity which I have drawn down upon wife and child, and many hundred friends and strangers, I renounce for ever happiness and joy, song, wine, and the love of women.

To the dead alone, slain for my crime, with whose ashes I here cover myself upon their grave mound, do I belong; and among the living, to my faithful blood brethren.

And if I break this solemnly sworn vow, then be Dame Harthild's curse wholly fulfilled."

And the stars and his friends in silence heard his vow.

CHAPTER X.

And Halfred kept his word.

Year after year passed away—he told me he no longer knew how often. Meanwhile midsummer returned—and Halfred lived a life which was as a living death.

Hartvik and Eigil commanded the Singing Swan, and ruled their sailing comrades. They chose the design, the port, and the course of their voyages. Halfred without word, wish, or choice, let everything be.

Only, when the south wind grew too strong for Hartvik's hand, Halfred strode silently to the helm, and steered until the sea was calm again.

Also, when Vikings attacked the ship, Halfred had forbidden that the Singing Swan, either by sea or land, should do harm to any—and the danger became overwhelming, Halfred silently—he raised the battle cry no more—grasped his hammer, and dashed among the enemy until they gave way.

But he wielded his hammer only with his left hand—his shield he had laid aside—and neither with helmet nor mail did he protect his head and breast.

And throughout the whole year he wore the garment which on that midsummer night smoke, flame and blood had darkly dyed.

When the Singing Swan drew near the land—the black flame marks on the wings none were allowed to efface—and Hartvik and Eigil and the sailors went to the halls of kings, Halfred stayed lying upon deck, and kept guard over the ship.

And he drank only water out of a cup of the bitter juniperwood.

Eigil brought once, from a king's halls where the Sigskald of yore had often been a guest, a splendid golden harp, which the queen, in greeting to her old friend, had sent as a present.

But as the ship turned out of the bay the harp, with a light rush, glided into the sea.

And once Halfred lay at midsummer in Iceland, on the shore by the black stone—for every midsummer night he spent alone there, his friends must remain on the ship—and looked very very sad. For his face had grown very pale.

Then there came a woman, and a wonderfully beautiful maiden, who was her daughter, and stood before him; and he turned away his face, but the

33

mother spoke—

"I know thee, even yet, Halfred Sigskald. I can never forget thy face, although the smile of Oski no longer plays thereon, and though the furrows on thy brow are deeply scored as with a plough. This maiden dids't thou, fifteen years ago, lay in my arms a sleeping child. See how beautiful she has become, as no other in all Iceland. And this wreath of summer flowers has she twined for thee. Set it upon thy pale brow, and thou shalt be healed, for gratitude has woven it."

Then Halfred sprang up, took the wreath from the beautiful blushing maiden's hand, lifted with mighty force the huge block upwards, threw the wreath under it, and let the black stone fall heavily in its place again.

The mother and maiden, weeping, departed.

And during these years Halfred spoke hardly to any, save Hartvik and Eigil, and to them only when he must.

And what he said was weak and mournful.

And his voice had become very low.

And he was very kind to everyone, above all to those below him.

And often in the night the sailors heard him sigh, and turn himself upon the straw bed upon the deck, where always, even in the cold winter, he lay under the stars.

And they heard him often speak when there was no one at hand with whom he could talk.

And at table he rested his head upon his left hand, and kept his eyes cast downwards, or looked into the far far distance.

And he almost never complained, only he often shook his head gently, and pressed very very often his left hand upon his breast, and said many times—

"The fresh air of heaven shuns me. I cannot breathe. If I will breathe I must sigh. My heart is almost crushed."

And Hartvik and Eigil said one to the other—"He is ill."

And once, when they sailed to Greece, Hartvik secretly called a physician —they are very skilful there—and the physician watched Halfred many days and nights, and said—

"It is a heavy malady under which this poor man suffers.

"And many have already quietly died of it, or sunk into madness.

"We call it 'Melancholy.'"

CHAPTER XI.

And the Singing Swan sailed again into the western seas, in the late spring and early summer, at the time which the Latins call "Mensus Madius."

And because of the long voyage the provisions were exhausted, and the ship also needed rest and repairing.

And Halfred's blood brethren said to him, when they came into the waters of the island of Hibernia—

"Both men and stores need caring for: we will land at King Thorul's sea castle, and provide all that we need on board. Far famed is King Thorul's hall; there they have great skill on the harp. Come with us to the city; rejoice thy heart in human fellowship, for there thou cans't not, as heretofore, lie upon the ship. Even to the Singing Swan will many people come, workmen and traders, and thou wouldst not be alone under thy stars. Shall we not steer for the green island?"

And Halfred nodded, and Hartvik joyfully turned the helm sharp to the west.

When, however, they saw the towers of Thorul's hall rise from the waves in the morning light, Halfred, with his own hand, lowered the smaller boat, which lay fastened on the deck near the helm, and said—

"When ye have rejoiced yourselves at King Thorurs court, and have provided for the ship, seek me, after twenty nights, on yonder small rocky island."

And he took arrow, and bow, and fishing hook, sprang into the boat, and rowed to the island.

But, the Singing Swan sailed further to the west.

And Halfred landed upon the small rocky island; he found a fitting bay, and drew his boat high up upon the white sand of the shore.

And then there came floating to him on the air something which was strange and yet well known to him. Only under the golden stars of Greece and Rome had he ever heretofore enjoyed the intoxication of such fragrance.

There is, that is to say, a flower of the delicate hue of a maiden's cheek, "Rosa" the Latins call it, and its fragrance is as the kiss of pure maiden lips.

And this flower had the Roman heroes, so long as they were powerful in these western lands, carefully tended in their houses and gardens. Long since, however, had the Roman heroes vanished, their stately dwellings were abandoned and ruined, their gardens grown wild.

And wild also had grown the maiden tinted flower which they call Rosa, and had spread all over the island, and flourished luxuriantly everywhere, and breathed forth a strong intoxicating perfume.

On these small islands which lie round about the great western island of Hibernia, the air is always mild; the snow seldom there remains lying on the land, and only slightly, and for a short time are the streams frozen.

And the singing birds which elsewhere retreat before the frost, rest for the winter in these retreats, where meadows, shrubs, and trees, remain green even in the severest seasons. For it rains often there, and moist is the breath of the billows rolling around.

And the heathen people, therefore, call these islands "Baldur's Islands," for Baldur they name the God of the spring dawning.

And as Halfred climbed up the hill from the shore, all the underwood and sweet-springing thorns were in full bloom; white thorn and red thorn and black thorn and the wild roses.

And also the many splendid fruit trees which the Roman heroes had brought with them from the south and the east, were in full bloom.

And from every shrub and tree resounded the sweet tones of the grey brown singing bird, which the Latins call "Luscinia," the Greeks "Philomela," but we, the "Nightingale."

And Halfred strode upwards and inland, by the side of a clear rapid stream, which flowed over white pebbles, through light green copsewood. On the height he came to a transparent copse of alders, young beeches, and slender white birches. There lovely broad-winged butterflies flitted over the beautiful flowers in the sunny glades. Deep in the thicket sang the thrush. The tops and pliant boughs of the birches nodded and waved.

And then there came to him, borne on the morning wind, yet other sounds than the song of the nightingale, far clearer and softer, as from the lightly-touched strings of a harp; but which sounded far more beautiful than any harp playing, either of his own or any other Skald, which he had ever heard.

And from high above, as if from heaven, the tones appeared to come. Halfred followed the sounds, which powerfully moved and allured him.

No sound since the last dying shriek of his harp had reached his soul through his ears. These harp tones aroused his soul. He believed that elves or Bragi, the song God, were harping in the air.

He wished not to scare the singer, but to listen. Softly he passed on, choosing his steps; the wood-grass betrayed him not, for it was soft, long, and thick.

He had now come quite near to the sound, yet still he saw not the singer. Cautiously he parted the thick white thorn bushes, and perceived then a small green mound, upon which stood in a circle six beeches. But the seventh, the tallest, stood in the centre, and towered above them all; and around its trunk wound an ornamental staircase made of white wood; and made of the same white wood there was a slight platform fitted in where the broad branches of the beech spread themselves out. The railing of both staircase and platform was ingeniously carved.

From this airy bower floated down the wonderful tones.

Halfred drew nearer, and spied through the branches and the crevices of the platform. His heart throbbed high with amazement, awe, and yearning.

There he saw the player.

On the railing leaned a boy who was wonderfully beautiful, so beautiful, Halfred said to me, that never had he seen such beauty upon earth—so beautiful as the elves must be, in which the heathen people believe.

He was altogether white—his slender face was white as the stone which the Greeks call "Alabaster;" the folded garment which reached from his neck to his knees was white, and white were the leathern shoes upon his feet.

But the eyes and hair of the boy were like gold.

And Halfred said to me that the eyes were the golden brown of the eagle's eyes. In the shining hair, however, which a net of the same colour confined, instead of a hat, played hither and thither, bright sun-tinted gleams, as though a sunbeam had lost itself therein, and now vainly sought to find an outlet.

And the boy played upon a small three-sided stringed instrument, such as only the Skalds of Hibernia carry, and played a wholly unknown melody.

And he played and sang so beautifully, that Halfred had never yet heard such playing and singing; mournful and yet blissful at the same time, was the melody, like the pain of yearning, which yet for no pleasure of the earth would the heart resign.

And Halfred told me that for the first time since that midsummer night a warm breath passed again over his soul.

And the beautiful boy in the airy bower enchained his eyes, and the mournful yearning song entranced his soul.

And for the first time, for many, many years, his breast could heave with a full drawn breath.

And tears filled his eyes, and restored and healed him, and made him young once more, like cool dew upon the heath after a burning sun.

And at the close of every two lines the words of the song rang harmoniously together, like—and yet again not altogether entirely like—as though two voices sought each other in sound and echo.

Or as when man and woman, one and yet two, are folded together in a kiss.

The boy sang in the soft lisping Irish language, which Halfred well knew. But that closing concord had he never heard, and it resounded far more pleasingly upon the ear than did the dead consonant staves of the Skalds.

And this was the boy's song,—

> "On light slender branches blowing
> White rose yearns through May's young bloom—
> Sun God, 'tis for thee I'm glowing,
> When wilt thou, thy bright face showing,
> Quaff full deep my fresh perfume?
> When wilt thou, for ardour sighing,
> Greet my flowers in trembling bliss?
> Come, and must I rue thee dying,
> Leave within my chalice lying,
> Fiery sweet, thy fervid kiss."

Here closed the boy's song and playing with a clear resounding chord on the strings.

And as soon as he ceased, and had hung his harp on the boughs, lo! there came flying from the nearest shrub two snow-white doves, which lighted one on the right, the other on the left shoulder of the boy, who smiling stroked their heads, and slowly, thoughtfully, with stately, and yet almost timed step, came down the white wooden stairs, and stood upon the beautiful flowery turf of the greenwood glade.

Halfred dreaded that he might terrify the gentle harper if he stepped suddenly out of the thicket before him.

Therefore he called to him first, from a distance, in a soft voice, slowly drawing nearer.

"Hail, gentle boy! If thou art mortal, may the Gods be gracious to thee. If thou art thyself a God, or as I surmise one of the light elves, then be not ungracious to me, a mortal man."

Then the boy turned slowly towards him, without seeming to be terrified, or even surprised, and as Halfred now drew nearer, he said in a melodious vibrating voice—

"Welcome, Halfred. Art thou come at last? I have tarried long for thee."

And he offered him both hands; the glance of the golden eyes sinking deep into Halfred's soul.

Halfred, however, dared not to touch those hands. He felt, from the very depths of his being, a quickening warmth uprise, and send rippling through body and soul a quiver of delight—of joy in surpassing beauty—but also of holy awe, as in the presence of gods or spirits; for he had no longer any doubt that it was no earthly being who stood before him.

Voice and breath almost failed him as he asked—

"Who hath proclaimed to thee Halfred's coming, and name!"

"The moonlight."

"Then art thou indeed, as I had already perceived, the prince of the light elves, to whom moon and stars speak words. Be gracious to me, O loveliest of the Gods."

Then the boy smiled. "I am a child of earth, like thyself, Halfred. Draw nearer. Take my hands."

"But who art thou, if thou art mortal!" asked Halfred, still hesitating.

"Thoril, King Thorul's orphan grandchild."

"And wherefore dwellest thou here alone, on this small island, as though hidden, and not in King Thorul's hall?"

"He dreamed thrice that danger threatened me, in the month when the wild roses blow; a strange ship which should come into his harbour would carry me away, never to be seen again.

"To render me quite safe against this danger he sent me here to this small outlying island, at which, because of its circling cliffs, no ship can land. Only Moëngal, his ancient armour-bearer, and his wife, my foster-mother, are with me; yonder, in that small wooden house, behind the beech mound, we live. But so long as the dear lord shines, and the gay butterflies flit over the flowers, I tarry here in hidden airy bower."

"But, thou wonderful boy, if thou art really a child of earth, how could the moon reveal to thee my coming and my name?"

"I sleep not in the moonlight, because it entices me out and upwards. It lifts me by force from my couch, and upwards to itself. With closed eyes, they say, I wander then away on the narrowest ridges of the roof; and far away, through forest and mountain, I see what shall happen in the future, and the distance.

"Carefully they guarded me, therefore, in the king's hall. But here, the clear moon looks freely through the rifts in our cottage roof.

"And I saw, seven nights ago, a ship, with a swan on the prow, that drew nearer and nearer. On the deck lay sleepless a dark-bearded man, with a noble countenance. 'Halfred,' his two friends called him.

"And ever nearer floated the sailing Swan. But when, one cloudy night, the moon shone not upon my pillow, and my eyes could not see the ship, and the man, then yearning seized upon me for that noble countenance. And I laid my pillow and my head, since then, ever carefully under the full flood of the moonlight. And night after night I gazed again on that lofty forehead and these palid temples.

"But still more beautiful and lordly art thou, than thy dream picture; and never have I seen a man to equal thee."

"But thou," cried Halfred, seizing both the singer's hands, "art like Baldur in spring beauty, gentle boy.

"Never have I seen such perfect charm in youth or in maiden. Like sunshine upon chilled limbs, like Chios wine through parched throat, flows thy beauty through my eyes deep into my soul. Thou art as the blackbird's song and the wood flowers: as the evening star in golden clouds; thou art as the most wonderful song which ever resounded from the lips of a Skald; thyself, as thou livest and movest, thou art pure poetry.

"O Thoril, golden boy, how gentle thou art! how thou hast quickened my grief-worn heart. O Thoril, leave me never again!

"Take up once more thy magic harp; uplift once more that sweet song, which has awakened my soul from the sleep of death.

"O come, let me lay my heavy head upon thy knee, and gaze in thy sunny wondrous face, while thou tunest thy harp, and playest and singest."

And thus they both did.

And trustfully flew one of the doves from Thoril's hand to Halfred's broad shoulder, and cooed lovingly to the other.

And when the song was ended, Halfred seized again the two hands of the boy, and drew them slowly slowly over his forehead, and his moisteyes.

And it all was as it stands written in the sacred books of the Jews, of the King full of sadness and heaviness, who could only be healed by the harp-playing of the son of Jesse.

CHAPTER XII.

And this lasted many days; and upon Halfred's forehead the lines and furrows disappeared, one after another. And once more he could draw a deep full breath without sighing.

And he carried his head again proudly erect, when he did not purposely bend down to look into the golden eyes of the boy, which ever again and again he did.

And so much did Halfred dread to lose Thoril again, that he never left his side the live-long day. And because Thoril's couch and sleeping chamber were, as he said, so small that Halfred could not share them, he lay before the door upon the threshold.

Nevertheless he still could not sleep; but now, because with ardent yearning he listened to the breathing of the sleeper. And with the earliest dawn of morning he would rouse Thoril from sleep and his sleeping chamber.

And it seemed as if the old gift of Oski was given back to Halfred, the winning of all hearts. For the two guardians of the boy, who full of mistrust had seen the strange man approach their cottage, holding Thoril's hand—the ancient Moëngal had rushed at him with a spear—were at once gentle and won, when he begged, with the old smile of Oski—"Let me be healed at Thoril's golden eyes."

But on the thirtieth day—the time when the Singing Swan should come for him was long passed, but Halfred thought not of that—the two went out with hooks and lines to catch fish. For Moëngal's provisions were exhausted.

In the midst of the island lay a dark lake, surrounded by steep high cliffs. But from the lake a streamlet flowed to the open sea. In a small boat they could row upon this lake, and down the streamlet to the sea. And there were many splendid fish called silver salmon in the lake, and in the stream, and even down in the salt sea.

And Halfred and Thoril rowed over the lake the whole morning, and laid ground hooks and nets.

And when, towards mid-day, the heat burned more and more fiercely down upon them, Halfred said—

"Come away from this shadeless depth. There above, on the cliff, I see falling the glittering spray of a silver rill—amidst alders, amidst wild roses it springs. There above, it is cool and shady. Easily shall we find a grotto in the rock. I long for that fresh spring water. And there above, to the left, nod dark sweet berries—they quench the thirst, and young boys love them. Let us climb up. I will gladly aid thee."

And slowly they climbed the steep face of the cliff. Thoril now aided, now followed by Halfred.

Then there floated to them, half-way up to the fountain, a strong perfume from a hollow linden tree, like wine, but it was wild honey which the wood-bees had gathered there.

And Thoril dipped his forefinger deep in the bright thick mixture, and laid it upon Halfred's lips, and smiled at him, and said—

"Take it. It is very sweet."

And most enchanting he looked.

Then Halfred exclaimed—

"Such honey, so say the people, the Gods have laid upon my lips. Try if it is true."

And he suddenly clapped Thoril's head, which was bent down towards him, with both hands, and kissed him on his full lips.

Then both started asunder. A burning glow shot through Halfred's frame. But Thoril turned away his face, quivering slightly, and rapidly climbed up the cliff.

Halfred paused, and drew a deep breath—

Then he followed.

"See, Thoril," cried Halfred halting, "this cavern, hollowed by the elves in the rock. The thick thorn bushes, with the perfumed red flowers, almost hide the entrance; and see there, how the brown nightingale on her nest guards the small doorway, and how the honey bees swarm around. Here will we stop and rest as we descend, when we have drunk above."

But Thoril made no answer, and climbed more quickly upwards.

They had still some fifty paces to climb upwards to the edge of the cliff whence the spring water fell in silver spray. Halfred was surprised that henceforward the boy went steadily on, turning his back to him, and if he sought to aid him in climbing, held on his course without looking round.

Fiercely beat the noontide down upon the cliff; all around was deep silence; only blue flies darted buzzing through the sunshine, and from high in the heavens sounded often the shrill cries of soaring falcons, which with outspread pinions circled over their heads.

They had now mounted so high that far away over the small island they could see, on three sides, beneath and around them, the blue sea appear.

And the sea encircled the blooming island with its dark steel-blue arm, like a mail-clad hero a blooming women.

But from the far west drew near a white sail.

At last they had reached the height. Thoril stood above, hard by the waterfall, where scarcely could a pair of human feet find standing room upon the wet slippery crumbling stone.

Beneath him, some five feet lower, Halfred halted, and looked towards him. "Give me to drink, I am parched with thirst," he cried to him.

And Thoril drew from his fishing pouch a curved, silvery shining, mother of pearl shell. He raised himself on tiptoe, filled the shell to the brim, and turned to reach it down to Halfred. Then his foot slipped on the polished stone, vainly he tried to save himself, spreading out his arms on the bare rock wall. Halfred saw him falling downwards, straight upon himself, and opened wide his strong arms to receive the light burden. But lo!—a miracle. In the rapid fall the buckle broke which fastened over the breast Thoril's white linen garment; wide outspreading, down over the shoulders, fell the garment; at the same moment fell the net which confined the golden hair—a rich flood of waving tresses spread themselves over the shining neck and swelling breast.

"A woman art thou? a maiden?" shouted Halfred exultingly. "Thanks to ye, O stars. Yes; this is Love's fullness."

And the beautiful maiden hid her glowing cheeks in Halfred's neck.

With a few strides he bore his light burden down to the grotto they had passed in climbing, and bending the branches of the rose bushes aside placed her safely within its shelter. The nightingale, which there sat singing on her nest, flew only to a short distance; and then returned and sang and warbled unceasingly. And the bees flew humming among the wild roses.

And when the crimson glow of the evening sun shone over the island Halfred and Thoril descended the cliff. And now the girl's face was infinitely more beautiful than of yore. She wore her hair no longer in the net, but waving freely, so that like a mantle spun of threads of sunny gold it covered her from her throat to her knees. And instead of the lost buckle a small spray of the thorn bush, with a full blown rose, fastened her garment over the breast.

Thus, hand in hand, they descended to the lake, and then Thora took from the boat her three-sided harp, and thus they wandered down by the streamlet which flowed from the lake to the sea, and on to the bay, towards the west.

And the ship, which from the west had held her course towards the island, was the Singing Swan.

There, at a short distance, she now lay at anchor in the bay; her sails shining brightly in the evening light. And the ship's boat glided over the water towards the shore, to bring Halfred and the smaller boat, rowed by Hartvik and Eigil.

And the blood brethren sprang on shore, and marvelled greatly, when they saw Halfred stand there, hand in hand with a wonderfully beautiful woman. Silently their glances questioned him.

But Halfred spoke, twining his arms round the slender girl—

"This is Thora the golden-eyed. King Thorul's daughter.

"She was hidden from me here, and clad in boy's clothing that I might not find her.

"Nevertheless I have found her, according to the course of the stars and the will of the Gods—Love her as myself—for she is my wife."

CHAPTER XIII.

And now it was very wonderful to see what a wholly different man Halfred had became since he had won Thora.

He threw off his tattered clothing, and clad himself in the most costly royal raiment of scarlet and rich gold, which lay stored away as a special treasure among the spoils of the Singing Swan.

He quaffed the sparkling Chios wine from a silver cup, and eagerly pledged Thora in Freya's love.

He played often upon her harp, and sang new songs far more beautiful and ardent, and moving according to a melody which he invented, and called "Thora's melody."

And his youth seemed to be given back to him, for the deep furrows vanished from his forehead, his eyes, which had always been cast down, as though he revolved the past, or his own thoughts, now looked brightly upwards again, and around his lips again played joyously the smile of Oski.

And he stirred not night or day from his young wife's side; and was never weary of stroking her long golden hair, or looking deep into her golden joyfully glistening eyes.

But in the night he often held her high aloft in his arms, and silently showed her to the silent stars.

And he had himself seized the helm, to turn the Singing Swan towards the south, for he said, "Thora shall see the islands of the blest, in the blue Grecian waters, where marble statues, white and slender as herself, look out from among evergreen laurels."

And the flame marks on the Swan's wings were effaced, and mast and spars must always be wreathed with flowers, for Thora loved flowers.

But the young wife had eyes for Halfred alone. She spoke but few words; but with sweet smiles she often whispered—

"Yes, verily, thou art the Son of Heaven. Mortal men, such as I have often seen in my father's hall, could never be at once so strong and so gentle. Thou art like the sea a furious irresistible God, and withal a lovely dreaming child."

And when she glided across the ship, all in snow white garments, and with her golden flowing hair, the men on the rowing benches sat with oars suspended, and Hartvik, at the helm, forgot to guide the ship's course, and followed her steps with wondering eyes.

And when they drew near to land, and the people saw her hovering on the wings of the Singing Swan—where she loved to stand—they brought offerings of flowers, for they believed that Frigg, or Freya, had sailed in to visit them.

And Halfred told me that she grew more beautiful from day to day.

And in this wise passed four times seven nights.

And Halfred was so infatuated and absorbed in Thora, that he did not in the least observe what was brewing among the sailors, or how his blood brethren, who held themselves aloof from him, whispered together.

He heard once, as he remembered afterwards that Hartvik whispered to Eigil, "No I tell thee. He will never do it himself, or by free will. Therefore the physician must by force burn out the wound from the sufferer."

He neither noticed nor understood these words. But soon afterwards he understood them.

One clear moonlight night Halfred and Thora had already sought their couch in their chamber between the decks, from whence a small gangway and flight of steps led upwards, and Thora had fallen asleep. Ere Halfred fell asleep however, it seemed to him as though he detected that the Singing Swan was, very slowly certainly, but perceptibly turning. She groaned, as though resisting the pressure of the helm; and he thought that he heard, through the open gangway, the sound of many steps upon the deck, and of whispering voices, and now and again of weapons clashing.

Instinctively he glanced towards the head of the couch; where his hammer hung, guarding his bride's pillow. The loop was empty. The hammer was missing.

Quickly, but lightly, so as not to wake the sleeper, he sprang up the narrow stairs. He was just in time. Hartvik and Eigil were in the act to close the small trap door, which fastened over the gangway with a bolt, and thus confine the pair between decks. There, now, stood Halfred, his right foot on the deck, his left on the highest step. Hartvik and Eigil started up, and drew back a pace. Hartvik was leaning upon Halfred's hammer. The ship's crew stood armed in a half circle behind him. The helm also was surrounded by armed men, and had been turned. The ship no longer sailed towards the south-east, but held west north-west, and the sails were half-reefed.

"What do ye here my blood brethren?" said Halfred, softly—for he thought of Thora—and was more amazed than angry. "Are ye mad, or have ye grown faithless."

For a while all were silent, startled at Halfred's sudden appearance, whom they had believed to be sleeping soundly by Thora's side. But Hartvik recovered and spoke—

"It is not we who are mad, or have grown faithless, but thou, our unhappy brother, under magic spell. We would have accomplished what must be done without it being possible for thee to hinder it. Thou shouldst only have trodden the deck again, when, against thine own will, thou wert restored to health.

"Now, however, since thou hast too soon learnt this, hear what we, thy blood brethren and the most of those on board, assembled in ship's council, last night resolved—resolved for thy weal, although many opposed it, and would first have spoken with thee. Submit thyself peaceably, for it is unalterable as the course of the stars, and although thou art very strong, Halfred Hamundson, bethink thee, thou art weaponless, and we are seventy."

Halfred was silent. Fearfully swelled his temple veins; but he thought of Thora. "She sleeps," he whispered. "Say softly what ye have to say. I listen."

"Halfred, our dear blood brother," continued Hartvik softly. "Thou liest spell bound in the toils of a woman who—I will verily not revile her, for I love her more ardently than my own heart's blood—whatever she may be, a mortal woman undoubtedly is not.

"Here works one of the strongest spells which ever witchcraft wove, and ever befooled the senses of men.

"I blame her not as do many of our comrades.

"She can do no otherwise. This is her very nature.

"She is in truth an Elfin woman, or what the Irish call their white half Goddesses.

"In the old Sagas it is told that there are such magic women, who, whether they will or not, wherever they come, bewitch the eyes and hearts of all men. In Herjadal lived such an one, seventy years ago, and there was no peace in the land until they had hung a mill stone about her neck, and sunk her where the Fjord is deepest.

"That this woman is no mortal woman can any one see who only looks once in her white face, through which all the veins shine blue, and in the selfish glittering golden eyes. This alone were enough, without that which many among us have seen; how, lately, when the moon was full, she rose unperceived from thy side, and floated up upon deck and with closed eyes danced up and down upon the slightest wing feathers of the Singing Swan, like an elf in the moon rays. And when the moon went behind a cloud she glided just as lightly down to thee.

"But this is the smallest part of her magic.

"Not thee alone has her beauty ensnared. She hath so crazed all the ship's crew that they forget work and duty to gaze after her as she floats along.

"Yes, even among us, blood friends, hath she kindled frightful sinister thoughts against thee, and against each other. I, who care not for women, and Eigil, who never thought of any woman save my burnt sister, we have lately by night confessed to each other that this silent white elf woman hath so fearfully crazed our senses, that each of us has already wished thy death, yes, would even have contrived it, in order to win this golden haired enchantress.

"And when we confessed these same thoughts to each other, we were filled with shame.

"Yet nevertheless each of us has plotted the death of the other.

"There must be an end of this.

"This slender sorceress shall not make men murderers in their thoughts, who have stood together through fire and blood.

"We will not throw her overboard, as many of the crew in superstitious terror advise. Where would be the use? She would swim like a sea bird on the tops of the waves. But we will bear her back to the lonely island, where no eye of man can see her, and where no doubt wise gods had banished her. We would all possess her, and none shall have what each covets."

Frightfully throbbed the veins in Halfred's temples, in his rage. "The first," he said, quite softly, through his gnashing teeth, "the first who lifts a hand, ay even a look towards her, I will tear his false heart from his living body."

And so frightfully threatening was his face to behold that Hartvik and all the armed men drew back a couple of paces.

But Eigil stepped forward again, and spoke in a louder voice than Hartvik had used.

"Halfred, give way. We have sworn it. We will compel thee."

"Ye compel me!" cried Halfred, also now in a louder voice. "Murder and revolt on board the Singing Swan! What saith the Viking code? Like a dog shall he hang by the neck at the mast head who secretly stirs up disobedience to the ship's lord."

"To the ship's lord, yes, when madness crazes him not," shouted Eigil again.

"Darest thou to speak of rights, Halfred Hamundson?

"Only because madness and magic excuse thee, have we not long since asserted our rights against thee: thou, who every word and bond of right hast broken. We demand our rights. But thou hast no right to that woman.

"Hast thou forgotten, Perjurer, that bloodstained midsummer night on Hamunds Fjord? Of that, in truth, thou hast not spoken, since, like a love sick boy, thou hast doted on this slender sorceress.

"Thou hast forgotten it, but the seamen who sail by yonder spot, they see with horror the huge black Heckla Stone which there hides an awful catastrophe, and covers a fearful curse. But huge and heavy as it is, it cannot bury it. Demanding vengeance the shades of many thousand dead arise, who lie there, through thy crime, and with whom thou hast broken faith and oath.

"For how did'st thou swear in that night?

"Here I renounce, on account of the awful calamity which I have drawn down upon wife and child, and many hundred friends and strangers, I renounce for ever happiness and joy, song, wine, and the love of women. To the dead alone, slain for my crime, with whose ashes I here cover myself on their grave mound, do I belong, and among the living to my faithful blood-brethren. And if I break this solemnly-sworn vow, then be Dame Harthild's curse wholly fulfilled."

"But thou carest no more for Gods or men, no more for us thy blood-brethren, who stood by thee to the death; who kept faith with thee against our own kindred; who defended thy head against King Hartstein's sword when thou layest defenceless as a child upon our knees; who for thee have slain our nearest kindred; for thee have given up sister and beloved.

"Her also, whose voluptuous lips have kissed forgetfulness upon thy forehead, even her also has thy selfishness forgotten; for thou wilt bring destruction upon her, as surely as the Gods hear curses, and chastise perjury.

"Doubtless thou hast never told the white armed enchantress what a fearful curse thou, with each kiss, art drawing down nearer and nearer upon her head."

"Silence, Raven," cried Halfred, threateningly, paling with rage and dread.

But Eigil continued, "Who knows if the golden eyes would not turn shuddering from thee did she know that upon thy head rests the curse of the wedded wife, burned through thee—of thy unborn murdered son. And thou hast exposed her as well as thyself to the fearful sentence—it will be fulfilled, for unerring is such deadly hate:

"'Cursed be thy proud thoughts—Madness shall strike them;

"'Cursed be thy false eyes—Blindness shall smite them;

"'Cursed be thy lying lips—They shall wither and smile no more;

"'Yet a twofold curse shall rend thee both, if thou winnest again a woman's love.

"'In madness and disease shall she perish whom thou lovest more than thy soul.'"

Here sounded a faint soul-harrowing moan from the open gangway.

"Thou here!" cried Eigil, and paused.

Halfred turned. There behind him stood Thora, not white as in general, but with crimson glowing head, like a poppy, her eyes gazing wildly upwards towards the moon and stars. Suddenly she uplifted both arms on high, as though to avert from Halfred's head some fearful stroke from the clouds. Then, once more, a faint but heart piercing moan, and she fell forwards upon her face, like a crushed flower. Blood flowed from her mouth. Halfred would have quickly raised her, but lifeless lay the slight form on his arms.

"Dead," cried Halfred, "murdered! And ye have murdered her!"

He let slip the ice-cold form, wrenched with one tremendous spring forwards his hammer from Hartvik, and swinging it on high, with one stroke of his arm brought it crashing down upon the heads of both his blood-brethren, so that brains, blood, and fragments of skulls were scattered all around.

With that deed began a slaughter on board the Singing Swan like that of the midsummer night; only it was much shorter, because there were fewer to slay.

It seemed to Halfred as though his temple veins had burst. He felt, instead of brains, only boiling blood in his head; he tasted blood in his mouth, he saw only red blood before his eyes. Without choosing, without asking who was for or against him, he sprang into the thickest of the crowd of armed men, seized man after man by the throat with his left hand, and shattered their skulls with the broad side of his hammer.

He did not in the least perceive that a handful of men stood by him. He did not notice the many wounds he received on arms, face, and hands, in close combat with his despairing foes. He raged on and slew, until all whom he could see before him lay dead and silent upon the deck. Then he turned, still brandishing his hammer, and shouted—

"Who besides Halfred still breathes on this accursed ship?"

Then he saw that some six men of those who had aided him kneeled behind him. They had formed, with their shields, a half circle round Thora's body, and had turned off many a spear which would have reached the form of the white sorceress. Halfred perceived this.

"Stand up," he said, with his left arm wiping away the blood and sweat from his forehead, and the white foam from his lips.

50

He thrust the blood stained hammer into his belt, and kneeled beside Thora, pillowing on his breast her face, which had become whiter than ever before.

"It was too much to bear and to hear at once. The frightful hailstones of this curse have struck the white rose too heavily."

Then she opened her eyes, and murmured, "Not for me, only for thee, have the horrors of this curse overwhelmed me."

"She lives! she lives! Praise to you, ye gracious Gods," exulted Halfred, "It could not be that she should die for the crimes of others. She must be healed, as surely as the Gods live. Had Thora perished for mine, for other men's guilt; with this hammer must I have slain all the Gods."

And tenderly and softly, as a mother a sick child, the mighty man raised his young wife in both arms, and bore her, treading softly, down the steps.

But once more before she left the deck, Thora opened her eyes. She saw Halfred stained all over with blood. She recognised, by their armour and clothing, the bodies of Hartvik and Eigil, with frightfully shattered heads. She saw the whole deck strewn with dead. She saw that only very few of the ship's crew were left, and shuddering, shrinking, she closed her eyes again.

CHAPTER XIV.

But Halfred kneeled day and night beside her couch. He held her languid hand; he listened to her faint breathing; he kissed from her lips the small drops of blood which often gathered there.

He had the board which closed the gangway between the decks taken away, and heaven and the stars shone down upon Thora's pillow.

When the day had gone ill, and much blood had flowed, and she fell asleep with the falling night, then he would mount a few steps, draw his hammer from his belt, and threaten the stars with furious words.

"If ye let her die for others' guilt, then woe to you, ye Gods, woe to all who live."

But had the sufferer gained strength, and smiled lovingly and peacefully on him; then this same ferocious man mounted upon the deck, kneeled down, and cried with outstretched arms, and tear-choked voice,

"Praise, praise, to you, ye gracious Gods! I knew it, verily, that ye live and rule justly, and would not let her die for others' guilt."

And if the day wavered between good and evil, between fear and hope, then he paced the narrow chamber with hasty steps and murmured inaudibly,

"Are there Gods! are there Gods! are there gracious Gods?"

And he believed that Thora heard this not, because she slept.

But she lay often awake, with closed eyes, and understood it all, and it troubled her sorely, in waking and dreaming.

And Halfred now told her, at her mute request, all about Dame Harthild, and the curse, and how all had happened.

When he had ended she murmured shuddering, "Much has been fulfilled! If yet more should be fulfilled, unhappy Halfred."

It seemed, however, that Thora was better.

And Halfred resolved at once to carry her upon deck, that she might breathe the fresh air, and again behold the beauty of sea and heaven.

And he had the deck carefully cleansed from all traces of the horrible fight, and ordered the sailors, the day before, to run into a coast which was bright with summer flowers, and commanded a whole mountain of flowers, as he said, to be piled upon the ship, for he would have her laid upon a hill of flowers.

And the men obeyed; and the whole deck was so thickly strewn with flowers that nowhere was a bit of wood visible.

And close by the mast rose a swelling couch of perfumed light wood-grass, and all the loveliest wood flowers, so high that it reached to Halfred's breast.

Over this he spread a rich white linen mantle, and laid the heavily breathing form upon it.

And again the moon was full, as on that night of the battle on the ship. But many storm-rent clouds were still driving across the heavens, and the sailing disk of the moon had not pierced through them.

And it was midsummer night. The first that Halfred had not spent by the black Heckla Stone in Iceland.

Thora had fallen asleep upon her flowers.

Halfred had covered her with his own mantle. And he sat close by the flower hill, and looked into the noble, pale, all bloodless face, and then quietly before him again.

"Ye have done all things well, ye merciful dwellers in the stars above. Ye have requited me, for that I never altogether doubted ye. I will not again question with ye, wherefore ye have ordained for me this second fearful thing, that I should be forced to slay my dear blood-brethren, and so many of the ship's crew.

"Because ye have saved this wonderful flower, and have not suffered her guiltless, to perish for other's guilt, for ever will I bless ye.

"And a song of praise will I compose for you, ye merciful and gracious Gods; such as never yet has resounded to your praise. Thanks to you, ye gracious Gods!"

And thus musing he fell asleep; for it was many many nights since he had slept.

Then a piercing cry awoke him, which seemed to ring from the stars. "Halfred." It fell upon his ear from high above.

He started up from slumber, and looked upwards. There he saw what filled him with horror. The full moon had, while he slept, pierced the clouds, and shone with full radiance upon Thora's face. Now Halfred saw her, standing swaying, high on the slender cross-spars, many many feet above his head.

Like a white ghost she shone in the moonlight; her widely opened eyes looked out into her future; her right hand she stretched, as though warding off, into the night. She did not hold fast by the slender towering mast, on whose giddying height naught else save the seabird, tossing, rested. And yet she stood firmly erect; but in her face was despairing woe.

"O Halfred," she wailed, in a low tone of heart-rending anguish, "O Halfred—how distracted thy looks—how fearfully tangled hair and beard! Ah! how thine eye rolls—and half naked—like a Berseker, in shaggy wolf's skin. And how stained thou art with the blood of guiltless men. And why threatenest thou the fair-haired shepherd the light-hearted boy? Beware— beware the sling—guard thyself—turn thy head—the swing whistles—the stone flies—O Halfred—thine eye." And bending far forward she stretched, as though she would protect, both arms into the air. Now she must fall—so it seemed.

"Fall not, Thora!" cried Halfred upwards.

Then, as though lightning struck, swift as an arrow, with a wild shriek, she fell downwards from the giddy height of the mast.

The white forehead struck upon the deck, her head and golden hair were bathed in blood.

"Thora! Thora!" cried Halfred, and raised her up, and looked into her eyes. Then he fell senseless with her upon his face among the flowers—for she was dead.

CHAPTER XV.

When Halfred raised himself again—he had already long since recovered consciousness, but not the power to rise—the sun was fast going down.

He called the six seamen, who had held themselves shyly aloof in the stern and lower deck, and spoke, but his voice, he himself told me, sounded strange to him like that of another person.

"She is dead. Slain for the sins of others.

"There are no Gods.

"Were there Gods I must have dashed out the brains of all of them, one by one, with this hammer.

"The whole world, heaven and sea, and hell, I must have burned with consuming fire.

"Nothing should any longer be, since Thora no longer is.

"The world can I not destroy.

"But the ships, and all that is upon it, I will burn—a great funereal pile for Thora.

"Do as I say to ye."

And he embedded with gentle hands, the dead Thora in the flower mound, so that almost nothing of her form and clothing were to be seen.

And by his orders the six men were obliged to bring upon deck all the weapons, treasures, clothing, and provisions, which were stored in the hold of the Singing Swan.

And Halfred heaped them around the mast upon the flower mound, and purple clothing, linen cloth, silken stuff, golden vessels, and soft cushions, he piled up all round about.

Then he poured ship's tar over all, and covered it with withered brushwood, and dry chips from the kitchen.

And he ordered all sail to be set—a strong warm south wind was blowing —

Then he mounted upon the upper deck, and overlooked all.

And he nodded his head, well satisfied. And then he descended to the kitchen, to bring up a burning brand.

When he came up again he found that the sailors had lowered the two ship's boats, the larger and the smaller boat, they lay tossing by the boat ropes, to the right and left of the Singing Swan.

"Hasten, my lord," cried one of the seamen to him; "so soon as thou hast thrown the torch, to spring into a boat; for rapidly, in this gale, will the Singing Swan flame up, and easily might the fire seize the boats, and cause both thee and all of us to perish."

Halfred looked with staring eyes at the man "Would ye still live, after ye have seen this?

"Think ye that I will live without Thora? after the guiltless for other's,— for my crime,—hath died?

"No, with me shall ye all on this ship burn—truly a worthless funeral pile for Thora."

"Thou shalt not destroy us, guiltless. Forbid it, Gods!" cried the man, and sprang upon Halfred, to wrest the firebrand from him.

But with a fearful blow of his fist Halfred struck him down upon the deck.

Laughing shrilly, he shouted, "Gods! Who dare still to believe in Gods, when Thora, guiltless, has died?

"There are no Gods, I tell ye.

"Were there Gods, I must have slain them all.

"And I will slay, as my deadly enemy, whosoever declares that he still believes in Gods."

Furiously he brandished the firebrand in his left hand, the hammer in his right, and cried to the trembling sailors—

"Choose—If ye believe that there are Gods, then I will strike ye down like this too forward comrade.

"But if ye renounce the Gods, then may ye live, and depart, and bear witness everywhere that there are no Gods.

"Are there Gods?" shouted the maniac, drawing near to the trembling men.

"No, my lord; there are no Gods," cried the men, and fell upon their knees.

"Then go—and leave me alone to my own will."

Quickly the seamen descended into the larger boat on the left.

Halfred, however, stuck the hammer in his belt, and strode with rapid steps hither and thither upon the deck, and set fire to mast and sail, and purple clothing and carved work, and to the neck of the Swan on the prow-wailing, the wind passed once more through the curved wings of the Swan.

The strong south wind fanned the crackling flames; quickly was the ship, on all sides, wrapped in a glowing blaze. The sails streamed like fiery wings from the mast.

Silently, with folded arms, Halfred sat upon the upper deck, his eyes rigidly fixed upon the flower mound.

Swift as an arrow flew the burning ship before the wind. The fire had rapidly consumed the dried wood grass, and Thora's form and face were fully visible. Then Halfred saw how the scorching flames seized upon Thora's long floating golden hair. "That was the last thing," he said to me, "that I saw for a long time."

In unutterable anguish he sprang up, and rushed all along the burning ship, straight through the flames, to Thora, He sprang upon the flower mound to embrace the body.

Then he felt a frightful blow upon his head, and left eye. The half burned mast had fallen with a crash upon him; he was dashed upon his face among the flowers and the flames, and darkness closed over him.

CHAPTER XVI.

When Halfred again awoke he lay in the bottom of a small boat, which drove over the open sea.

His hammer lay at his right hand. A cruise of water stood at his left hand. Two oars were in the stem of the boat.

Halfred started up to look around him.

Then he perceived that he could only see with difficulty what was on his left side. He felt for his left eye, and found a bleeding cavity. A splinter of the mast had struck it out, and a stabbing pain beat through his brain, which he said never again left him as long as he lived.

He looked at his body. In charred rags his burnt clothing hung upon him. Far in the distance he saw a craft which he recognized as the larger boat of the Singing Swan.

The Singing Swan herself had disappeared; but away to the south there lay a cloud of vapour and smoke over the sea.

The boat in which Halfred stood he recognised as the smaller boat of the Singing Swan. Evidently his sailing comrades had dragged the half-burned maniac from the burning ship, and saved him.

They had abandoned him to the Gods whom he had blasphemed, and in whom they believed, to be saved by them, or perish. But no more fellowship would they have with a man stricken by the heaviest of curses—madness.

For mad Halfred was, from the hour when he sprang into the flames, and the mast struck him, until shortly before his death.

Therefore could he only tell me very little of all that in the meantime happened either to, or through him.

But what he did tell me, here I faithfully write down.

But many many years must he have wandered in madness.

He told me, moreover, that he saw only before his eyes how Thora fell from the mast; and how the flames seized her head and hair. And that he could only think one single thought. "There are no Gods. Were there Gods I must have slain them.

"So must I slay all human beings who believe in Gods; for blotted out from the earth shall be the name and remembrance of the Gods."

And he could not die until he had slain the last man who still believed in the Gods.

And thus he journeyed all about, everywhere, in his small ship; landed in bays and upon islands, lived upon game which he hunted, or upon domestic animals which he found in the fields, upon roots and wild berries from the woods, upon eggs of sea-birds, and mussels from the rocks.

And often the storm waves broke high over his boat, and shattered her planks. But she sank not, nor was he drowned.

And one day he saw he was wholly naked, the last charred rags had fallen from him. He was chilled, and when he met a wolf in the wood, he ran after him so long that he overtook him, slew him with his hammer, took off his skin, and hung it round his loins.

And thus he roamed and sailed, half naked, all about the north. And none recognised in the maniac Berseker, Halfred Sigskald, the son of Oski.

And he told me that when he chanced upon mankind, whither they were many or few, he sprang upon them, and shouted to them his question.

"Are there Gods?"

And if they said "Yes," or as the most did, gave him no answer, then he slew them all with his hammer. But if they said "No," as also many did—for it was already rumoured throughout the whole north, that a naked giant wandered through all lands with this question, whom the people called "God destroyer"—or if they took to flight, then he let them live.

And often, from dread, the peasants and the women gave him fruit, bread, milk, and other food. Many however bound themselves in a league to go out and slay him, as a wild beast. But they could not stand before the fury and strength of the maniac. He killed the bold, the timorous fled.

He slept hardly at all at night, therefore they could not surprise him in his sleep.

Once, when he spent the night in the bam of a peasant, who had previously renounced the Gods, with all his household, the people from the court barricaded the straw-filled bam, and set fire to it. But Halfred burst through the roof, dashed through the flames and arrows, which could not pierce his body, and slew them all with his hammer.

And this maniac wandering endured many years.

And sea storms, and burning suns, and autumn frosts, and winter ice, beat upon Halfred's half-naked body.

And his hair and beard stood out like a mane around him.

But no longer dark, as when of yore he trod, as a wooer. King Harstein's courts—but snow white. In a single night—the night when Thora died—his hair had become white.

CHAPTER XVII.

And after many years he came sailing in his rotten boat over the seas which play around the island of Caledonia. He landed, seized his hammer, and strode upwards to a steep rocky hill, on which sheep and goats were grazing.

It was early morning, in the time when roses begin to bloom.

Mist floated over the sea, and upon the cliffs.

Then Halfred saw the shepherd standing above, on the cliff's edge; and he played a lovely melody upon his shepherd's pipe.

And at first he doubted whether he should ask this shepherd boy his question about the Gods, for he left women and boys unquestioned. And this shepherd seemed to him but a boy.

But as he climbed nearer to him he saw that the shepherd carried a spear, and a shepherd's sling, with which to kill wolves.

And the shepherd lad believed that this was a robber or a Berseker coming against him and his sheep.

And he chose out of his leather pouch a sharp heavy stone, and laid it in his sling, and held it ready to cast it.

Halfred held his left hand over the eye that remained to him, and looked upward with difficulty, dazzled, for just then the sun broke out through the mist clouds exactly above the head of the shepherd, who thus saw clearly the figure of the half naked man, with tangled floating hair and beard, who now raising the hammer threateningly ascended the hill. Upon a slab of stone, under a great ash tree, he stopped, and cried to the shepherd—

"Are there Gods, shepherd boy? Sayest thou yes, then thou must die."

"Gods, there are not," replied the shepherd, in a clear voice, "but wise men have taught me there lives one Almighty Triune God, Creator of Heaven and Earth."

The man with the hammer paused for a moment as if meditating.

Such an answer had he never received.

Soon, however, he sprang threateningly upwards again.

Preventing him, however, the shepherd swung his sling; whirring flew the sharp stone; it was a sharp hard three-edged flint stone—I had carefully reserved it for some great peril—and alas! alas—woe is me, only too truly did it strike. Without a sound Halfred fell, where he stood, on his back under the ash tree, himself like to a suddenly felled tree.

With a few bounds the shepherd reached the prostrate form, cautiously holding his spear before him, lest the enemy should suddenly spring up again. For it might be that he only artfully feigned to be wounded.

As he drew nearer, however, he saw that it was no deceit, but rather evident truth.

Blood streamed over the fallen man's right cheek, and in the cavity of the right eye stuck the sharp flint stone.

But pity mingled with dread seized upon the shepherd, as he gazed in the fearful mighty face of the man who lay mute at his feet. Never before had he seen so splendid a face; at once so noble, and so sad.

And superstitious fear overcame him, if it might not be the chief of the heathen gods, Odhin, the one-eyed, who in the semblance of this wanderer with the white beard had appeared to him.

But soon he felt yet deeper sympathy and compassion, for the wounded man in a weak voice began:—

"Whosoever thou mayest be, who hast cast this stone, receive the thanks, O shepherd boy, of a world and woe weary man. Thou hast taken from me the light of the second eye also. I need no longer to see men-kind and the heavens. Neither of them have I understood for a long time. And soon shall I pass to where questions are no more asked, and curses no more cursed. I thank thee, whosoever thou mayest be. Thou hast of all living beings—save one—done the best for Halfred Hamundson."

Then with a loud cry I threw my spear on one side, fell upon my knees, embraced the pale bleeding head, and cried:—

"Halfred, Halfred, my father, forgive, forgive me!—I am the murderer— and thy son—"

Now ye who shall one day unroll this parchment—pause at this place, and look upwards to the sun, if it is day, and to the stars, if it is night, and ask with Halfred—"Are there Gods?"

For I, I, who secretly and in dread write these pages during the night hours, I am the shepherd boy, Halfred's son, who have slain him.

And the Gods, or the Christian God, have allowed it to come to pass that the son has blinded and murdered the father.

I wept hot tears upon my dear father's pale forehead. But he turned his head, as though he would see me, and said—

"It is hard that the curse must be so wholly fulfilled upon me, that I must be entirely blinded before death.

"Fain would I have looked closely into thy face, my dear son.

"Now I know not if the golden cloud I saw spread about thy head was thy hair or the sun rays.

"Thou seemedst to me fair to look upon, my boy.

"But tell me, how do they call thee?

"Have they verily, at thy birth, named thee Liarson Scoundrelson Harthildsvengeance? and how did it happen that thou camest into life. I believed Dame Harthild burned in the dwelling house."

Then I laid my dear father's head upon my knees, and dried with the long yellow hair I was at that time still allowed to wear, the blood from his cheek, and told him all.

How my mother would not be carried from the burning Mead hall back into the dwelling house, but rather on to one of the ships of her father.

How from thence, when the battle and the flames threatened dwelling house and ships, she was borne by her women and the sailors into a boat, and therein rowed out upon the Fjord.

How in the boat she had forthwith given birth to a son, but died herself; and ere she died had laid her hand upon my head, and said—

"Not Liarson—not Scoundrelson—not Harthildsvengeance shall he be named—no; Fridgifa Sigskaldson."[6]

"She was right in that," said Halfred. "Thou hast aided the Sigskald to peace at last."

And how after she was dead the fearful battle and burning on shore scared the sailors and women still further out to sea.

And how the small boat was almost sunk by the fury of a storm from the west, and all the bondmen and women were washed overboard by the waves, save one rower, and a bond maiden, who hid the infant under the stern seat.

And how, at last, Christian priests, who were sailing out to convert the heathen people, picked up the half starved wanderers, and brought all three hither, to the island of the holy Columban; and cleansed both the two, and the infant, with the water of baptism.

And how the two, my foster parents, told me all that they knew about my father, and mother, up to the time of the burning of the Mead hall.

And how the two were never weary of lauding to me my father's glory in battle and song.

And how the monks of Saint Columban, as I grew, would have me taught to read and write; but I loved far better to go out with the hunters and shepherds of the monastery, and liked to draw targets on the parchment leaves for my little cross-bow.

And how, at length, they declared me unfit for books, when with my small bolt I had pierced through and through a costly picture which on the gold ground of a thumb broad margin represented the whole of the Passion, and promoted me with a sound thrashing to be herd boy of the monastery.

And how for many years, since my foster parents were dead, I had kept the sheep of the monastery; and my sole pleasure therein had been in fighting with the bears, the wolves, and the eagles, that attacked the lambs.

Or in playing upon my shepherd's pipe, or in listening to the roar of the sea and the forest.

And Halfred laid my head upon his broad breast, and folded both his arms around it, and laid his hand upon it, and was still and silent for a long time.

And I brought him water to drink from the fountain, and milk from my flock; and would have drawn the stone from the wound, but he said—

"Leave it, my dear son—the end draws near.

"But I feel the band taken away from my brain, which for many many years has pressed upon it.

"And all becomes clear and bright to my thoughts. I can see inwardly again how all has been, now that I can no longer see outward things.

"And for thee, and for myself, before I die, I will set forth clearly and exactly how all has been. Give me once again milk from thy flock to drink."

And I gave him to drink, and he laid his head again upon my knee, and began to tell me, quite clearly and distinctly, all that had come to pass since that midsummer night.

And from his lips have I learned all, onward from that midsummer night, which in the earlier pages of this book I have written out. And much have I also learned from him, of those earlier times of which my foster parents could know nothing.

And I have kept it all in faithful remembrance.

And as the evening fell he came to the end of his account, and he said,

"Lay my face so that once more the sun shall shine upon it. Fain would I feel the dear Lord once again."

And I did as he commanded.

And he breathed deeply, and said:

"It must certainly be spring. A perfume of wild roses floats to me."

And I told him that he lay under a blooming rose-bush.

And then a blackbird raised his sweet song from the bush.

"Thus I hear once more the blackbird's evening song," said Halfred.

"Now farewell all. Sun and sea, forest and stars of heaven, wild rose perfume, and songs of birds; and farewell to thee, my dear son. I thank thee that thou hast released me from madness, and an evil life.

"I can, to requite thee, as all my heritage, leave thee only this hammer. Guard it faithfully.

"Whether there be Gods—I know not. Methinks that men can never search it out. But I tell thee, my son, whether Gods live or not, hammer throwing, and harp playing, and sunshine, and the kiss of woman, these are the rewards of life.

"Mayest thou win a wife who is but a faint reflection of Thora.

"Then hail to thee, my son!

"Bury me here, where mingles the roar of the forest and the sea.

"Farewell my dear son. Dame Harthild's curse thou hast turned for me into a blessing."

And he died.

The blackbird ceased singing in the bush. And as the sun sank, one warm full flood of his rays streamed full upon that mighty face.

Thus died the son of Oski.

CHAPTER XVIII.

When now my dear father was dead, whom I myself had slain, I wept bitterly, and lay all night by the side of the dead.

And when the sun again arose I considered what I should now do.

At first I thought I would drive the flock to the monastery, which lay some six stages distant, and relate all to the monks, and confess how I had, all unwittingly, slain my own father; and beg for absolution for myself, and for a Christian grave for my dear father.

But I bethought me that the monks would not bury my father with Christian honours, since he had died a heathen. And neither would they allow me to burn him, after the custom of the heathen people, because the heathen gods would thus be brought much into remembrance. And they would certainly throw him, unhonoured, into the sea, as they had already done to a heathen from Zealand.

So I resolved to be silent about it all, and not to betray my dear dead father to the priests.

And thus could I neither confess the death blow, nor receive counsel respecting my guiltless crime.

And from thence was the beginning of my freeing my mind from the monks and their creed.

And I knew, quite near, of a cavern, which was known only to me, for it had a very small entrance, and I had only discovered it because I had followed a stone marten which had slipped into it. A fallen block of stone concealed the entrance, and I found many ashes and remnants of bones within the spacious cavern, which opened towards the sea. In early days, no doubt, the heathen Scots had burnt their dead here. Thither I carried, not without much difficulty, my dear dead father, and set him upright in the cavern, his face turned towards the sea. The roots of the oaks and ashes which waved above the cavern, penetrated through the stone downwards almost to his head. Above him roared the forest, before him roared the sea. There did I place my dear father, and rolled the stone again to the entrance.

But even his hammer, his only possession, I dared not keep. Even should I tell the monks I had found it, or bought it from sailors—they would not have left it with me, for strong heathen victory runes were engraved on the haft.

So I laid then the hammer also close to the right hand of the dead. "Guard it for me, dear father," I said, "till I need it again. Then will I fetch it."

But from that hour there came a great change over my disposition.

That which had most delighted me, to fight for my sheep with wolves, bears, and birds of prey—that attracted me no more.

Rather the question which had driven my dear father even to madness, if there be a God, or Gods? And how it could be that such fearful things should come to pass as are here set down in this history, from the vow upon the Bragi cup, on to this great horror, that the son had slain his own father. These questionings seized upon me, and would not let me rest, any more than my dear father.

And as my dear father of yore looked up to the stars, and implored the heathen Gods for enlightenment, so also did I look up to the stars for illumination, praying to Christ and the saints.

But to me also the heavens were dumb.

Then I said to myself—"Here on the sheep pastures, and from the roar of the sea, and from the light of the stars, wilt thou find no answer all thy life long, any more than thy dear father.

"But in the books of the monks, the Latin ones and those others, with the crinkled runic flourishes, lie hidden all holy and worldly wisdom.

"And when thou can'st read them, all will be clear to thee in heaven and upon earth."

And so I took leave of my dear father, gathered my sheep together, and drove them to the monastery.

"Art thou gone mad, Irenæus?" asked the porter, as he opened the door for me and my bleating charge, "that thou drivest home before shearing time. They will scourge thee again."

"I was mad," I replied, "but now I will become a scholar. Now another may scare the wolves. I will learn Greek."

And thus I also said to the good Abbot Aelfrik, before whom I was at once led for chastisement.

But he said—

"Lay the scourge aside. Perchance the boy, who has always been a heathenish worldly Saul, has become suddenly a Paul, through the grace of the holy Columban. He shall have his wish. If he holds to it—then it is a work of the saints. If his zeal flags, then it is a wile of Satan, and he shall go out again to his sheep."

But I kept silence, and said nothing about the reason for which I wished to learn.

And my zeal did not flag, and I learned Latin and Greek, and read all the books that they had in the monastery, the Christian ones of the church fathers, which they call theology, and many heathen ones, of the old world wisdom, which they call philosophy.

And I soon perceived that often, in one church father, was found just the contrary of what was in another church father.

And that Aristotle reviled Plato, and that Cicero tried to make sense of it all, and could not.

And after that I, in three, four years, had read through all the books which they had in the monastery, and had contended all night long with all the monks in the monastery, I knew no more of that which I wished to know than on the day when I had buried my dear father.

The old good-natured fat Abbot Aelfrik however—he was of noble race, and had formerly been a warrior at the court of the Scottish King, and loved me—often said to me,

"Give up these searchings Fridgifa"—for he willingly called me by my heathen name when we were alone. "Thou must believe, not question. And drink often, between whiles good ale or wine, and sing a song to the harp"— for he had taught me harp playing, in which I had great delight, and which he loved much, and everyone said that none could play the harp like me in all Scotland; "and forget not either often to throw the lance at the target in the monastery garden. Much book reading withers the body."

And I remembered that my dear father's last words had been just the same. And often and often I stole away to my dear father's hill, brought forth the hammer, exercised myself in hammer throwing by star light, and sat then for hours before the cavern, and listened to the roar of wind, wood, and wave.

And now it often seemed to me as if, in such moods, I came nearer to the truth than through all the books of the Christian priests, and heathen philosophers.

And I almost believe I shall not stay much longer in the monastery.

Especially since, lately, a skald from Halogaland visited the monastery, and told of the life at the court of King Harald; of his lordly royal hall, in which twenty skalds by turns play the harp.

And how the boldest heroes ever willingly enter his service.

And how year by year his warlike expeditions are crowned with victory.

And of Gunnlôdh, his wonderfully beautiful golden-haired daughter, who pledges the bravest heroes and the best skalds in the horn.

Since then, my inclination no longer turns towards psalm-singing and vigils.

But certainly they will not easily let me leave the monastery.

For because I can write Latin and Greek well, Aaron, the new Abbot, the Italian, who has succeeded the good peace-loving Aelfrik, makes me unceasingly write out manuscripts, which they then sell for a great price, in Britain, and even in Germany.

And Aaron is very sharp upon my track, because I seem to him to lack true Christian zeal.

And did he know that upon these parchment sheets, whereupon I ought to have written out, for the seventeenth time, the treatise of Lactantius "de mortibus persecutorum," I have, by night, written out the history of my dear father—it would not pass without many days' fasting, and some score of penitential psalms.

Lately he actually threatened me to have "some one" scourged, who ever again came too late for the Hora.

That "someone" was I. For I had just begun to write about the battle on the Singing Swan, and could not tear myself away from it when the Hora bell called.

But ere the son of Halfred the Sigskald endures scourging on the back,— rather will I slay Aaron and all his Italian monks.

But for slaying I need something different from this copying style.

*   *   *   *   *

Thus far had I written by Good Friday.

For a long while could I not contrive to write further. For the hatred, jealousy, and mistrust of Aaron and his hangers-on—there are many of his Italian countrymen come with him from Rumaberg—grow constantly greater. He has forbidden me to write by night.

Only by day, and in the library, no longer in my cell, may I write. And the transcript of Lactantius I am to deliver to him on the appointed parchment by Whitsuntide, on pain of seven days' fasting.

My resentment increases against this priestly tyranny.

Only rarely, and by stealth, can I get at these pages. Also I can only with great difficulty reach my dear father's hill. They track my lonely wanderings.

It will soon come to open war. At any rate I will provide myself with a sure weapon.

*   *   *   *   *

With difficulty did I, yesterday evening, in the sleeve of my frock, bring my dear father's hammer into the monastery. I have hidden it in the outer court, but where—that I do not trust even to these pages. I think much over the question of my dear father, and I believe that soon I shall find the truth.

*   *   *   *   *

For three days I could not write at all. The skald from King Harald's court has again been a guest in the monastery.

I have made him tell me all about the life at that court. It is just as in my dear father's days. Certainly King Harald and all his courtiers are heathens, and their warlike expeditions are mostly against Christian kings and bishops. But that does not make me waver in my purpose, which is firmly resolved. He told me much about Gunnlôdh.

In twenty nights a ship of King Harald's will sail again into the harbour from...

*   *   *   *   *

I know now the answer to Halfred's question.

There are no heathen Gods.

But neither is there any Christian God, who, almighty, all merciful, all wise, allowed that the father should be slain by the son.

Rather, that only happens upon earth which is necessary, and what men do and do not, that must they do and not do; as the north wind must bring cold, the south wind warmth; and as the stone thrown must fall to the earth. Why must it fall? No one knows. But it must.

But men should not sigh and question and despair, rather rejoice in hammer throwing and harp playing, in sunshine and Greek wine, and in the beauty of women.

For that is a lie that it is a sin to long for a beautiful woman. Otherwise must the human race die out; if all become so devout as no more to long for a woman.

And the dead are dead, and no longer living.

Otherwise had the shade of my dear father long since appeared to me, at

70

my earnest entreaty.

Of what alone, however, man should believe; of that I will speak hereafter.

Without fear shall he live, and without hope shall he die.

In this monastery, however, will I remain no longer than—.

CHAPTER XIX.

Thus far had he written, the God forsaken Brother Irenæus. Here fell the righteous judgment of Heaven upon him.

I, Aaron of Perusia, called by the grace of God to feed these lambs of the holy Columban, had also the grace given to me to drive the diseased sheep from the flock.

Long was I on the track of him and his worldly, heathenish, sinful, ungodly, yea God-blaspheming doings; his guilty conscience had rightly boded this. Step by step I had him watched by Italian brethren, full of godly zeal, without his observing it. The most pious of them, Brother Ignatius of Spoletum, succeeded in winning his confidence—for stupidly unsuspicious are they—these barbarians—through often allowing him to entertain him with harp playing, Irenæus begged from him one day some ink powder from his store, as he had used up his appointed portion, and from the "Head of the Pharisees"—thus the shameless sinner termed his abbot and chief shepherd—could not obtain fresh supplies, without delivering over what he had written with the former supply.

Brother Ignatius at once, as was his pious obligation, told all to me, his abbot. But the ink powder he gave to him, with that wisdom of the serpent which is well pleasing to God in his priests.

Soon thereafter the sinner set out again upon one of those secret expeditions which have ever been his wont, remaining out the whole night when some errand had allowed him to escape from the monastery. I never forbade him to go out, for I hoped through one of these secret expeditions, most easily to discover his hidden doings. I sent, spies after him every time; but every time he suddenly and mysteriously disappeared among the wooded crags along the shore.

This time I myself sent him out, and as soon as he had left the monastery court I at once made a most rigorous search through the whole of his cell.

There at last I found, after much labour, these blasphemous pages, written very small, in his accursed graceful handwriting, and artfully hidden in a crevice between two stone slabs of the floor.

I took the devil's work with me, and read and read, with growing horror. So much sin, so much worldliness, so much heathenish delight in fighting and singing, in drinking and carnal love, so much, finally, of doubt, of unbelief, of naked blasphemy, had, under the roof of the holy Columban, under my pastoral staff, grown up, and been written out!

Abhorrence seized upon me, and holy indignation.

Forthwith I summoned the Italian brethren to special secret council and judgment. I pointed out to them the deadly poison of these writings, which indeed were full of the seven deadly sins; and the unanimous sentence was pronounced. First, three hundred lashes with the scourge; then immuring in the chastisement cell, with vinegar, water, and bread, until repentant contrition and the fullest amendment were made manifest.

Impatiently we awaited the return of the accursed sinner.

With the vesper bell he entered the door of the monastery court.

Immediately I placed myself before the door, shot the iron bolt, and called forward the Italian brethren. The greater number, the Anglo-Saxons, who were well disposed towards the blasphemer, on account of his sinful harp playing, and lukewarm in zeal for the Lord, I had before collected in the refectory, and locked up until the offender should be secured.

Hastily the Italians came, and behind them several armed bondmen of the monastery. Then, in place of all accusation, I held up these pages before the miserable wretch, and pronounced the agreed upon sentence.

Then, ere we were aware, the God-detested criminal sprang with lightning speed to the cistern in the court, and drew forth from behind it a frightful horrible hammer.

"Dear hammer of Halfred, aid his son today," he cried in a threatening voice.

And the next thing was—it seemed to me as though the Heavens fell upon my head and neck—I sank upon the ground.

Only after a long while did I awake again.

Then I lay upon my bed, a man given up, and the brethren from Italy lamented around my couch; and recounted that the furious Samson had, with a second blow, shattered the bolt on the door, and made his escape. The monastery servants, indeed, followed him, and several of the brethren, led by brother Ignatius. But when the fugitive suddenly turned, and slew the foremost of the pursuers, one of the monastery servants, who would have seized him, with the frightful hammer, and struck down brother Ignatius, severely wounded, the others gave up the pursuit. At once he again disappeared, as always, among the cliffs and woods.

Never have we seen him since, although from the very day of my awakening I had him carefully searched for all along the coast. The cavern of which these accursed pages speak could we not find. I would have had the bones of the old heathen murderer thrown into the sea. Probably the son concealed himself there, until he could leave the island on some ship. I however, in consequence of the blow from his hammer, which shattered my shoulder and collar bone, on one side, have to suffer all my life long from a hideous twist of the neck, which is exceedingly prejudicial to the dignity of an abbot.

This sinful book of abominations however, I sent to Rome, to the holy Bishop, with the question, whether we should burn it, or preserve it, to aid in tracing and convicting the escaped monk, should we succeed in capturing him again?

For a long long time came no answer.

But after many many years the book came back from Rome, with the command to keep it—only the blasphemous passages therein were erased—and as a warning example to others, was the Abbot of St. Columban to append to these pages an account from an accompanying letter of the Archbishop Adaldag of Hamburg, of how dreadful a fate had, through the righteous judgments of God, ended this apostate's sinful life of the highest earthly enjoyment; which he—this may console us—will doubtless have to expiate in the eternal torments of hell.

From the Archbishop's letter it appeared there could be no doubt that our perjured Brother, Irenæus, is none other than one who, in all the courts of the north, has been for many years celebrated as a warrior and singer, and crowned with all earthly fame and happiness, Jarl Sigurd Halfredson; who appeared suddenly at the court of King Harald of Halogaland—none knew whence he came—with one of the skalds of the King, and through hammer throwing, and harp playing, soon won for himself such renown that King Harald gave him three castles, the command of all his armies, and his daughter Gunnlôdh in marriage.

But King Harald was the most furious Christian hater, and the bitterest opposer of the Gospel in all the North.

And for long years Jarl Sigurd led the troops of King Harald, and always led them to victory.

The Lord at that time tried his own with severe affliction. He had turned his face from them, and the vassals of the Bishops, and of the Christian princes of the North, could not stand before Jarl Sigurd, and his dreaded hammer.

But the end of this man of blood was horrible, and therefore it has been—

by the command of the holy Father—copied from the letter of the Archbishop, as a fearful warning to all who read these pages.

As he, that is to say, after once more in a great battle overthrowing the Bishop's troops, was pursuing them in sinful joy, and shouting "victory, victory!" he was mortally wounded by an arrow in the breast.

King Harald caused his heathen priests and the skalds to draw near to the right side of the death bed, to console him with songs of Valhalla.

The wounded man waved them away with his hand.

Then drew near, on the other side of the dying, three Christian priests, who had been made prisoners in the battle, and would have given him the holy last Sacrament, if he acknowledged the Lord.

Indignantly the godless sinner repulsed them with his arm. And when King Harald, astonished, asked him in whom then he believed, if not in the heathen Gods, nor in the white Christ? he laughed and said—"I believe in myself, and my strength. Kiss me once more, Gunnlôdh, and give me Greek wine in a golden cup."

And he kissed her, and drank, and said—

"Glorious it is to die in victory"—and died.

But he remained unhonoured and unburied by heathen priests and Christians, since he had defiantly rejected both.

So then it is certain and set forth as a warning to all—but to us a righteous consolation—that the God accursed soul of this most blasphemous of all sinners must burn in hell for ever and ever—Amen.

POSTSCRIPT.

What I here wrote down, years since, as my belief concerning the fate, after death, of this abandoned sinner, has been fully confirmed by a delightful testimony.

That is to say, Brother Ignatius—who lately died—and certainly in great sanctity—was before his death honoured by a wonderful vision.

Saint Columban, himself, in a dream, led him by the hand into hell, and there he saw, in the deepest pit of sulpher, Brother Irenæus, burning whole and entire.

But upon his left shoulder blade, on the spot where he struck me, his Abbot, sat an infernal raven, and hacked unceasingly through the shoulder even to his blaspheming heart.

Of this has Brother Ignatius assured us before his death. And therefore have I hereunto add this also, about the raven and the shoulder blade, in order that all who read these pages, but especially the disciples of the holy Columban in this monastery, may learn the chastisement which awaits him who lifts heart and hand against his soul's shepherd, the Abbot.

AMEN.

Lightning Source UK Ltd.
Milton Keynes UK
UKHW011832240521
384311UK00001B/171